Of the River: A Collection

by

Lucia V. Delgado

Beyond Borders Books

Pharr, Texas

Of the River: A Collection

Copyright © 2025 Lucia V. Delgado

ISBN: 979-8-218-79389-0

Beyond Borders Books

Pharr, Texas

beyond-borders-books.com

Publishing Acknowledgements: "La Posada" was previously published in Issue II of *Common Forms*

Cover design by Analisa Estrada

First Edition, Printed in the United States of America

Delgado, Lucia V.

Of the River—1st edition.

Lucia V. Delgado

ISBN: 979-8-218-79389-0 (pbk.)

I. Title.

Fiction, Family, Code Switching, Southern Border, Texas, Northern Mexico, Rio Grande Valley.

For Rory, as promised

ACKNOWLEDGEMENTS

Time stretches and shrinks when you write a book. Publishing my debut novel took six months, four years, a lifetime. It took a childhood and adolescence spent nestled against a crook of the Río Grande. It wouldn't have been possible, were it not for the people who raised me.

I want to first thank my family. My mom and dad, my brother Eric, my Tía Lorena, Tío Jaime, Tía Aida, and Tita. I would not be the person that I am without you guys—thank you for giving me such a rich history to pull from. Thank you to Caro, the first person to tell me that I should write about Brownsville. Thank you to my scores of little cousins—I'll see you at the next Posada.

Thank you to the countless educators who have shaped me as a writer. To Ms. Beth Garza, who read every installment of the Dancing Peanut Saga when I was eleven years old. To Dr. Alice Batt at the University of Texas, who forever changed the way that I approach writing. Last but never least, Ms. Ruth Poole—thank you for my magnifying glass necklace and my curiosity. So much of what I know of life and love and loss, I learned from you.

Thank you to all my dear friends, who cheered me through the best of times and pulled me through the worst of times. Thank you to Cooper, Hannah, and Raishma for reading every version of every story in this collection. I could not ask for a better workshop group. Thank you to the indomitable Diana Fierro, for always picking up the phone. Thank you to JR, for shooing me away when I needed to just go write the damn book. And thank you to Vince, for reminding me that I did not, in fact, write it by accident.

Thank you to Thomas Ray Garcia and Beyond Borders Books for taking a chance on my debut. Thank you to Analisa Estrada for designing such a lovely cover.

And to everyone left unmentioned… if I've loved you, you are in here; if you've loved me, you'll forgive it.

The Dog on La Calle Solernau

Matamoros, Tamaulipas

2004

The summer days were long, and getting longer still. For Cacahuate, it just made it even harder to find a comfortable scrap of shade to lie under.

Cacahuate was, by anyone's measure, a dog. No breed in particular—just a brown dog with a white belly and a half-torn ear. He belonged to no one, yet everyone at once. He traipsed through the streets of the border town of Matamoros—migrating from one neighborhood to the next as his mood pleased him. But, since early spring, he had found himself staying closer to this one street near the center of town, La Calle Solernau.

Although he did not belong to the family in the yellow house, it had become his most frequent haunt. And, though he still enjoyed the freedom of the average Mexican street dog, he found himself unwilling to stray more than a day's walk from its orange awning and stone planter boxes. He liked it because, if he waited long enough, the old man who owned the house would come outside to feed him leftovers in a paper towel.

"Ten, perro vagabundo," he would say, as he scratched Cacahuate behind the ears.

Mostly, though, Cacahuate stuck around for the old man's grandchildren, a boy and girl of four and seven years. Though they lived three miles north, on the other side of the Mexican-American border, Cacahuate saw them often. Every weekday during the summer months, their mother would drive them across the Rio Grande to stay at their grandfather's house. Every morning, Cacahuate watched as the woman carried her still-sleeping children into the yellow house. More than once, he saw her wring her hands as she walked back to her car. She worried, though Cacahuate could never fathom why. The children were happy at their grandfather's house, so far as he could tell. Though, admittedly, his observations of the children often revolved around their willingness to bring him food.

Esther-Alicia was still the baby of the family then. She carried a stuffed animal everywhere she went and snuck Cacahuate Cheerios out of the stash she always kept in her pockets. She was quick to cry, but also quick to laugh. Though she often tried to climb onto Cacahuate like he was her noble steed, and he did not appreciate such behavior, he still had a soft spot for the little girl with tangled hair and sleepy eyes.

Her brother, Emiliano, was a bit of a different story. He was only seven years old, but tended to act older than his age. Cacahuate once heard his grandfather tell him that, with the situation on the border being what it was, he was going to have to grow up sooner than his older cousins had.

"Sé fuerte, pa tu hermanita," the old man had said. Though Emi tried his best to be a man, whatever it was that meant, his attempts mostly resulted in him puffing out his chest and taking charge of situations he really had no business taking charge of. Like trying to get a street dog into a collar…

But Cacahuate liked the children, regardless of their faults. He watched them often, from his place on the porch, where the shade was pleasant and he had an elevated view of the street. As the summer went on, he learned their patterns. How every day, after lunch, when the sun just barely began its descent from the highest point of the sky, the two of them would come out to play on the stretch of road in front of the house.

The siblings tried their best to alternate who picked their games, as per their grandfather's instructions, but Cacahuate soon saw that there were only so many hours that Emi could play make-believe before growing frustrated with his sister. If he ever went as far as trying to push or shove her, however, a low growl from Cacahuate was enough to set him straight.

There was a time, near the middle of summer, that Alicia always insisted on playing what she called the Detective Game, in which they would "solve the mysteries of the block"—primarily by using notepads to write down the comings and goings of the neighbors. The children would choose different houses to stake out, write their notes, and report back to each other. Though nothing ever came of their investigations, they spent several afternoons with their heads bent over their notes, discussing the pattern of Mrs. Aldrete's grocery runs and how the Martinezes three doors down had come home with a brand-new car that they drove all the way to San Antonio to buy.

Their grandfather put an end to their game, however, when he caught the children peeking over a cinder block fence to look into a neighbor's backyard. He warned them that nothing good ever came from being nosey.

"Tú a lo tuyo," he said to his granddaughter, as she sniffled and held her notepad close to her chest. The old man pressed his lips together tightly, not wanting to disappoint her, but fearful of what might happen if the children caught sight of something they shouldn't. "We have to be careful, beba. We don't know who lives here anymore," he said quietly, kneeling to look her in the eye.

But it was summer, and disappointments were fast forgotten. The children found other ways to keep busy. More often than not, Cacahuate found that their games devolved into sibling rivalries: who could run from one light post to the next the quickest, who could kick a soccer ball the farthest, who could pile the most tajín onto their tongue without needing water to wash it down.

One day, around the end of July, Emi and Alicia decided to test who could climb over the iron gate the fastest. Because of the recent uptick in break-ins, the old man had installed a fence to cage in the front yard. Wrought iron and several feet tall, its bars ended in sharp points that seemed to stab into the belly of the hazy summer sky. It was meant to be imposing, but, to the children, it was just another passing adventure. For Cacahuate it was a bit of an inconvenience, as he no longer had access to the porch and the lovely shade it had once provided.

Regardless, Cacahuate watched from the street with interest. Despite the exposure to the worst of the summer heat, he still preferred to stay close by. That day, he watched Alicia make quick work of the gate. She kicked off her shoes, scampered to the top of the fence, and slid back down the other side—only slightly burning her palms in the process. Emi tried to follow suit, but made the mistake of looking down when he reached the top. Seized by fear and vertigo, his sweaty hands slipping, he did not jump lightly from the fence so much as fall away from it, several feet in the air.

He landed on his knees—hard. At first, he didn't make any noise at all. Just stayed on the ground, seemingly frozen into place. But, when Cacahuate went over to inspect him, he saw that the boy was using his mop of dark hair to hide the tears in his eyes. His breaths were rapid as he tried to keep himself from crying.

Cacahuate was unsure of what to do. He was, after all, still a dog. But he felt compelled to move forward and press his wet nose against the boy's leg. This, apparently, did not help at all. Emi shoved him away none-too-gently. Cacahuate fell backward, trying not to slip on the hot sidewalk. Quickly, he regretted having gotten involved at all.

"¡Vete! Pinche perro!" The boy said, biting his lip hard enough to draw blood. By then, Alicia had recovered enough from seeing her brother fall to be upset by this.

"¿Pa que hiciste eso? He didn't do anything to you!" she shouted, planting her feet in front of Cacahuate and crossing her arms, all stubborn defiance.

Emi said nothing to her, but Cacahuate felt that he wanted to. He wanted to ask her to go get help, but couldn't. Wouldn't. Cacahuate understood. When fighting dogs in the street, you couldn't lick your wounds until after the fact.

Still, a dog has his honor. Cacahuate ran through the alleyway and towards the back of the house. The backyard was fenced in as well, but Cacahuate pawed at the wooden gate and barked as loud as he could. He had no way of knowing if he'd be heard, but he had to hope that the old man was within earshot.

After a few minutes, and a considerable amount of scratches gouged into the already-peeling paint, the gate finally swung open. The old man must have been in the kitchen because he walked out with a ladle in one hand and half of a lime in the other. Though his eyes were sharp with anger, Cacahuate gave him no opportunity to act. He merely barked once and ran. The old man followed close behind, cursing the damned dog under his breath.

In the embrace of his grandfather, Emi finally allowed himself to cry. Though his knees hurt so badly that he could barely bend them, that stopped mattering when the old man swept him up in his arms and carried him inside for bandages and agua fresca.

Cacahuate did not attempt to follow them inside the yellow house. He was content to stretch out on the sidewalk and fall asleep to the sounds of the children helping their grandfather in the kitchen. The children were safe, and perhaps they'd even learned a lesson.

. . .

A few nights later, long after the children had gone home, Cacahuate was startled awake by the sound of squealing car brakes. He had fallen asleep with a chicken bone wedged between his paws and had to stand up to physically shake off his disorientation. He stood to attention, though, because the car was not one he recognized. This wasn't Emi and Alicia's mother bringing them over for a visit. The woman who stepped out of the car and slammed the door shut behind herself was a stranger. And a distraught one, at that. He thought of barking to get the old man's attention, but one look at the woman's determined expression told him it was not his place to intervene.

After much insistent ringing of the doorbell, the old man finally made an appearance.

"Santiago," the woman said, in the place of a greeting. The old man looked up and down the street twice before even meeting her eyes. When he finally deemed it safe, he pulled her behind the gate.

They got all the way to the porch before he spoke. Cacahuate had to

press his snout between the bars of the gate to see them clearly.

"Raquel, ¿qué pasó?" Santiago was pacing, and Cacahuate

could smell his fear from several feet away.

The woman, Raquel, didn't respond at first. She was shaking,

and her gaze had become unfocused. Santiago had to repeat his

question several times before she answered. Even then, Cacahuate

could barely make out her response.

"Vi-vinieron en la noche. Ni sabía—no tenía idea… no sé

cómo…" Her words were halted by her shaking breaths. When she

broke down in sobs, Cacahuate had to shy away from the gate. Her

cries were gut wrenching and her words were so pained. Even the little

brown street dog knew that something was very, very wrong.

They spoke in hushed tones for a while, and Cacahuate perked

up his left ear, the torn one, to make out bits and pieces of their

conversation.

"Tienen a mi hijo. Tienen a mi hijo y quieren dinero y no sé

qué voy a hacer," Raquel said, her voice a strained whisper.

Cacahuate felt, more than heard, Santiago's weary sigh. The old man rested a comforting hand on the woman's shoulder and pulled her into an embrace. He waited a long while before finally speaking again.

"Ellos—los narcos—te quieren asustar. Quieren que pienses que tienen más poder que lo que realmente tienen. Una llamada, un cheque, y tu silencio. Es todo lo que necesitas para ayudar a tu hijo."

With that, Cacahuate decided that he had heard enough. He got up and walked away to find another sidewalk to sleep on. Things on his street were changing, and Cacahuate wished they would stop. Santiago's grandchildren used to be his constant, but even that wasn't true anymore. In the past two weeks, Cacahuate had noticed a change in their routine. Where Emi and Alicia's mom used to bring them to their grandfather's house at dawn, before work, they now came during her lunch break. Where the family used to stay late on Friday nights for carne asada, the children were now taken away before the first hint of sunset. All of the adults were on edge, it was only the children who continued as if nothing had changed.

Cacahuate walked for a long while that night.

. . .

The week before the new school year began, Emi and Alicia's mother proposed a day trip to Boca Chica Beach. The children were ecstatic, of course, but they also insisted that she let them bring Cacahuate along.

She had eyed the dog warily. He had fleas, though not many, and his fur was coated with a fine layer of dirt and grime that he had acquired from enthusiastically rolling around in the dusty streets. She wanted to refuse outright. Unfortunately for her, however, she had raised two incessant children. Soon enough, she relented, though not before insisting on a bath.

And that is how Cacahuate found himself tied to a fence post with a length of clothesline wire, with two children dumping bucket after bucket of soapy water on him. He put up a fight, at first, but he gave in to their persuasion just like their mother did. After a few bites of a hotdog, he was successfully bribed into standing still long enough to be scrubbed out of his hard-earned stink.

"Mom says we might not be coming back to Tito's house for a bit," Emi said thoughtfully, as he worked clumps of mud out of Cacahuate's front paws. He'd been making an effort to practice his

English. His teacher even mentioned that, if he worked hard enough, he should be able to speak without an accent soon enough.

"Por la escuela?" asked Alicia, who was too young to share his concerns about the lilt of her voice.

"I think so. Pero no sé. She said to make sure we took all of our toys home this time. All of your stuffed animals."

"Y el Nintendo?"

"And the Nintendo,"

"But we'll be back for Día de los Abuelitos, no?"

"Of course. And Día de los Niños."

"And Christmas."

"And Año Nuevo."

The siblings shared a smile, grateful that they had so much to celebrate. So many reasons to come home. Their mom might have moved their family north, but it was only three miles that separated them from the country they knew. Just the banks of a shallow river. A stone's throw, in the eyes of a child.

After they had loaded everything into the car, Cacahuate kept an eye on the Rio Grande as they drove over the old bridge. He had never seen the river before, and he was surprised by how wide it seemed. The water was so calm that he could see an entire mirrored world in it—the bridge, the reeds, and even the walls that towered over either side. He figured he could swim across it if he really wanted to. But, when he saw the tanks and men and guns that waited for them on the other side, he decided that he very likely did not want to.

The drive to Boca Chica Beach was a short one, but Cacahuate and Alicia still dozed off together in the back seat. Alicia slept with her little hands tangled in Cacahuate's brown fur and her nose nestled against his neck. After the car pulled into the sandy parking lot, the two of them stood around, drowsy and useless, as Santiago and the mother unpacked.

Cacahuate lifted his brown nose up to smell the ocean. The clash of sea-salted air and hot asphalt should have been jarring, but he found that he liked the scent. He was sometimes able to pick up hints of it in Matamoros, when the wind blew the right way. But, on the beach, the smell was just there for the taking. He breathed deeply, wanting to commit it to memory. As much as a dog is able to commit to anything, of course.

When he'd finally had his fill, he realized that Alicia had toddled forward—towards the ocean, but also toward the street where cars full of people sped by from one beach access to another. Panic seized him, and he rushed forward after her. He butted at the back of her legs, trying to get her out of harm's way as quickly as possible. When they finally crossed the street and Cacahuate looked back, however, he realized that there was not a car in sight. Alicia laughed and reached down to pat him on the head. She knew nothing of the tragedy that could have occurred and thought the poor, anxious dog was just as excited to see the water as she was.

The sea fascinated Cacahuate. Waves curled around his paws, beckoning him forward, and he tasted salt with every breath. Alicia laughed as he chomped at the tide, gagging with his attempts to bite at the saltwater.

It was the best day in Cacahuate's short memory. He ran up and down the length of the beach for hours, chasing children and the tide and the setting sun. He ate everyone's sandwich crusts and lapped up the water that Emi poured for him out of a metal canteen. He sat by patiently while the children built their sandcastles, and joined in when they decided that it would be more fun to destroy them.

After he finally tired out, he sat at the foot of Santiago's foldable beach chair and stayed with the old man as they watched the rest of the little family from afar. Cacahuate wagged his tail as the old man scratched him behind the ears.

"Ya? Finalmente te domesticaron?" Santiago chuckled to himself. "Supongo que ya no te crees tan vagabundo. Cuidalos, por favor."

Cuidalos. Take care of them. For all his attempts to maintain his street-dog freedoms, he realized that those two kids had managed to domesticate him, after all. At that moment, when Cacahuate heard Alicia squeal after falling face-first into wet sand and he instinctually stood to attention, he realized that it wasn't necessarily a bad thing. He wasn't alone anymore. The children were a part of his pack, and he had every intention of taking care of them. Of helping them through the cuts and scrapes and whatever it was that made their mother wring her hands with worry. He wanted to be like the iron fence that Emi once fell from, that which shielded them from the dangers of the world. On the car ride home, Cacahuate made his decision.

He would be their protector.

What he did not know, however, was that their mother had already made her decision, too. The violence had escalated one unsolved case too far. The border wasn't safe. The days of dual citizenships and dual lives were behind them. The children never came back to la calle Solernau. They never spent another summer playing in the streets and drinking aguas frescas. They would not return for Christmas, Día de los Niños, or even Año Nuevo. Not for many years.

Cacahuate never saw them again.

La Posada

Brownsville, Texas

2023

Esperanza Mendoza de Garcia had been making champurrado all afternoon. Her red-tinted hands smelled like the dozen cinnamon sticks she had cracked between them and dark chocolate stains covered her checkered apron. Esperanza was old, nearing her 84th year. Her eyesight was failing her, her hands swelled with arthritis, her memory was not what it used to be, but she would always remember how to make champurrado for her family.

She stood alone in the kitchen. Soon, the house would be flooded with people. Her seven brothers, their collective twenty-eight children, and their forty-one grandchildren. The halls would be filled with music, laughter, and the scent of decadent holiday food as everyone gathered for La Posada—Esperanza's most treasured family tradition.

La Posada was an annual party that landed two weeks before Christmas and celebrated the biblical story of Mary and Joseph finding shelter in Bethlehem. The night was one of food, games, piñatas, and a sing-along reenactment put on by the youngest of the grandchildren. It was the only night of the year that all three generations of the family were guaranteed to gather.

All seventy-six loud and loving members of the Mendoza family.

Preparations for the party had started early that morning. Her daughter, Celia, decorated the entire house with twinkling lights and garlands, and her two eldest granddaughters, Xiomara and Sofia, spent the afternoon making tamales. Esperanza had watched them assemble the tamales from the stove, where she carefully stirred the chocolate-cinnamon beverage. The two of them paid her no mind, they were deeply engrossed in their conversation, but it made Esperanza happy to see them together again. Xiomara had gone far away for college— far enough that it made no sense for her to return to Brownsville before now. But now she was home and warm and safe and Esperanza had every intention of filling her up with champurrado and family time before she sent her back to Oregon.

The doorbell rang, and Esperanza made her way toward the front door. She wiped her hands on her stained apron and straightened up as best she could, though her spine creaked with the effort.

"Entren, entren ¡Bienvenidos!" Esperanza greeted the first guests, her brother Romeo and his wife Rocio. She could see their daughter Roxanna struggling to drag a plastic bin across the driveway. Esperanza was about to shout over her shoulder for Xiomara to come help, but then she saw that her grandchild was already on her way over.

"Ahí voy, ahí voy," Xiomara said under her breath. She stopped to drop a quick kiss on Esperanza's cheek before greeting her Tía and Tío and going out to help Roxanna.

"Was there no line at the bridge?" asked Esperanza, as she ushered Romeo and Rocio into the living room. They lived five miles south, on the other side of the Rio Grande, and would have had to cross the International Gateway Bridge to come into Brownsville.

"Pos si, it's always bad this time of year, pero we left Matamoros pretty early."

"Que bueno, and did you bring the candles pa la Letanía?" Esperanza asked eagerly.

"Like we do every year? Of course, hermanita." Romeo reached out and squeezed his sister's hands. Esperanza barely had enough time to serve them steaming mugs of champurrado before the doorbell rang again.

This time it was Tetito, her nephew Humberto's oldest child. He moved up to Colorado a few months ago, and Esperanza smelled the lingering evidence of that in the acrid scent that clung to his winter coat.

"Ernesto Ivan Mendoza Cantú!" Esperanza admonished him, giving him a little sapo upside the head as he sheepishly tried to move past her.

"Ay Tía it's not what you think! Fue un zorillo, I swear."

"Uh-huh, seguramente. Tell your Tito what I think of your skunk when you see him." Esperanza continued to chastise him, but with no real fire behind her words. She was distracted soon enough when she felt someone place an infant in her arms.

"¿Y quien es este chiquitin?" Esperanza asked, gazing down at the baby's sweet brown eyes.

"That's Tómas, Tía. You met him at Xiomara's graduation, remember?" Esperanza looked up to see the baby's mother, Beatrice. Bibi was the youngest daughter of Esperanza's youngest brother. Though Esperanza was technically Bibi's aunt, the girl was only two years older than Xiomara.

"Sí, of course," she said softly, "little baby Tómas." Esperanza drew the child close to her chest, breathing in his newborn scent.

She rocked the baby softly as she led Bibi into the living room. Already, the festivities had begun… y también el desmadre. Rocio unpacked and unfolded the costumes that the children would use later in the night. She shook off the dried grass from last year and bemoaned the mud on the hem of the baby-blue Mary costume. Xiomara set out in search of some club soda while Roxanna and Tetito bickered over who got to select the music. Sofia squealed from the top of the stairs when she saw her older cousins and raced down to greet them. The chatter rose above the music (Roxanna won, and put on a cheerful Christmas playlist) and an aura of familial comfort settled over the room.

It was the night of the Posada, and Esperanza was content.

…

Xiomara Gonzalez Mendoza was one tamale away from committing a murder.

She should have stayed on campus for Christmas break. She knew she should have. And she would have, if not for her mother's insistence that she come home for the Posada.

"Como te atrevas a romperle el corazón a tu Tita?" her mother had asked her, as though her grandmother didn't have nine other grandchildren to keep her busy.

She tried to resist, but Xiomara was easily guilted—it came with the fact that she had already devastated her family by deciding to move out of state for college. Her parents wanted her to come home, so she did. But she should have known better. If she had given it an ounce of critical thought, she would have realized that her mother, Celia, simply wanted to cast off some of the pressure that came with organizing the biggest Mendoza family gathering of the year.

As the eldest daughter of the eldest daughter, Celia was expected to host the Posada at her house every year. As *her* eldest daughter, Xiomara had to do all the grunt work that the party entailed. Already, she had been asked to put up the Christmas lights in the backyard, sweep the front porch, pick up trays of desserts from the panadería downtown, and get a pot of pozole going on the stove. With the help of her younger sister, Sofia, Xiomara had spent the better part of her afternoon assembling and steaming dozens upon dozens of tamales. She knew it would be weeks before she stopped smelling masa every time she washed her hair.

It wasn't the act of making the tamales that bothered her. In fact, she quite enjoyed spending a few hours in the kitchen with her sister. She called Sofia often while she was at college, but it was always better to hear her stories in person, to hear of her homecoming dance fiascos and friend group conflicts. Sofia had always had a flair for the dramatic, and she regaled her high school escapades with a slew of exaggerated impersonations and dramatic pauses. The time passed quickly once the two of them got their little tamalada going.

The problem didn't start until a good two hours into the party. Once the bulk of the Mendoza family had come through the front door—scores and scores of Tías, Tíos, primas, and primos—the time came to serve the food. Celia was busy sorting through the props and costumes that would be needed later in the night and Sofia was off wrangling the little cousins, so it fell on Xiomara to start putting together the plates.

It was fine at first. Xiomara started as tradition dictated, by serving the oldest members of the family: her grandmother, her great-uncles, and all their respective spouses. All of them thanked her graciously and took a few moments to ask her about her time at college or comment on how delicious the food looked.

It was the second generation of Mendozas that grated her.

Xiomara had always enjoyed the presence of her Tíos, her mother's brothers and cousins, when she was a kid. They drank plenty of beer and danced to Tejano music and always hoisted the little ones up on their shoulders when it came time to hit the piñata. Their jokes were a bit ill-timed on occasion, but their laughter was booming and contagious. However, now that Xiomara was a lot older and a little more educated, she found it difficult to ignore some of their more distasteful habits.

None of the Tíos thanked her when she brought them their plates of food, they just continued in their conversations. They snapped their fingers when they wanted more Miller Lite and didn't even look at her as they took the beer bottles. Xiomara gritted her teeth, but continued to serve them. She figured her mother would at least want her to wait until after the little ones got to sing La Letanía before she picked a fight.

Xiomara was in the kitchen, fetching Tío Mando's fourth beer and chatting with Camila, who had just arrived, when Sofia barreled into her. She almost dropped the amber bottle in her hand when she tried to catch the edge of the counter for balance.

"Mom's on a rampage. Avoid the dining room if you can," said Sofia, in a loud conspiratorial whisper.

"Chin, what happened this time?" Xiomara asked, already trying to spot an obvious problem she could take care of before their mother got too frantic.

"Güey, what do I know? I'm avoiding the dining room. I think I heard something about a cake?" Sofia shrugged unceremoniously and left out the patio door into the backyard.

Xiomara rolled her eyes, but she couldn't blame Sofia for wanting to get the hell out of dodge. This party, as fun as it was supposed to be, stressed their mother out within an inch of her life no matter how well it went. There would be no shortage of calamities before the end of the night.

Besides, Xiomara had her own battles to fight—the ones that came in the form of middle-aged Mexican-American men.

She reached her boiling point when she saw what the Tíos were doing with the hojas. Xiomara's mother had left a bin on the back porch where everyone could leave the discarded corn husks from their tamales so that they could be composted later. Even though the bin was clearly labeled and Xiomara had been calling out reminders all night, the Tíos proceeded to just toss their hojas away with the rest of their trash. When Xiomara chided them, they waved her off with a dismissive, "No hagas tanto guato, mija, es una fiesta!"

Right when Xiomara was about to bite back, she felt a warm hand press down on her shoulder. She turned and saw her Tío Santiago, her grandmother's youngest brother and her favorite of the great uncles.

"Oye, cabrones," Santiago scolded the men, "I don't know who raised you to be tan maleducados, pero seguramente no fui yo. Apologize to the girl and do whatever she wants you to do o vamos a tener broncas." Santiago leaned in close. "Keep this up, and the two of us are going to spit in your next round of beers, me entienden?"

The Tíos muttered their apologies, not meeting each other's eyes. It had been a while since they had been so thoroughly chastised, and they didn't quite know what to do with themselves. Xiomara, on the other hand, grinned widely as she and Santiago walked back to the kitchen.

"Gracias, Tío, you have no idea how much it means to me. I've been dealing with them all night and I swear I was about to get violent," Xiomara said, as she picked up the tongs and started stacking even more tamales on a fresh paper plate.

"Don't mention it, cariño." Santiago smiled at her kindly and took the plate from her hands. "And give me this. You've done enough for tonight, yo me encargo de esto. Sit down and have a cold cheve for me, I promise not to tell your Mami," he whispered, winking.

Xiomara didn't need to be told twice. She grabbed an empanada de cajeta on her way out of the kitchen, dug a beer out of the bottom of an ice chest, and found a seat at a table reasonably far away from her mother. For the first time the whole night, Xiomara finally relaxed.

…

Sofia Gonzalez Mendoza was in over her head. She was running out of ways to entertain the little ones, and they were beginning to mutiny.

For the last five years, Sofia had only one responsibility during the Posada—to keep the little ones, the grandchildren on the younger side of her generation, busy. It used to be a straightforward endeavor. She would either turn on the TV and have them watch old Cartoon Network reruns or supply them with puzzles and coloring books from the dollar store. However, the Mendoza family popped out at least two new babies a year, and it wasn't long before "the little ones" became a group of twenty-plus kids whose ages ranged from toddlers to twelve.

Sofia started the night by leading all the kids into the yard. She half-hoped that would be enough for them and they would keep themselves busy. Factionalism set in quickly, though, and the kids couldn't decide on what to do. The girls wanted to play make-believe and had already started coming up with a long and convoluted plot line about being orphaned puppies with superpowers—or something to that extent. The boys couldn't be bothered, they just wanted to throw sticks at each other until someone caved and started crying. Collectively, they all turned to Sofia and demanded entertainment.

"Do something," urged Diego. He was twelve years old and the eldest child of Tío Mario. As their self-appointed leader, he was just old enough to question Sofia's tentative sense of authority. Sofia had liked Diego well enough when he was younger, but the onset of middle school and an addiction to red Gatorade gave the kid an entitled attitude that Sofia wasn't particularly fond of.

"What do you want me to do?" Sofia asked, crossing her arms.

"Play a game with us or something," Diego insisted, the rasp in his voice dragging out the last syllable.

"What game do you want to play? Tag? We can play tag," Sofia offered diplomatically, "or hide-and-seek."

Diego clicked his tongue, "Nobody plays tag anymore. But, whatever, I guess."

Sofia suppressed an eye roll. Nothing annoyed her faster than a kid with an attitude who had just learned how to wield the word "whatever."

"Come on, let's go." Sofia walked over to the anacahuita tree at the edge of the yard. "I'll be 'it'; the tree is base; you guys get a five-second start."

The group of kids all gathered close to the tree. The youngest of them were excited, just happy to be a part of the game. Diego muttered to himself but participated anyway. Sofia counted down slowly, "Five…four…three…two… ONE!"

She sprinted after the nearest kid, Lucas, and ran a circle around him before tapping him lightly on the shoulder. He squealed in delight and ran to tag his younger sister, Susy, who wasted no time in tagging her brother right back, and Lucas managed to tag Michelle when she tripped over a tree root.

The game went on for a while. Any time a little cousin chased Sofia, she tried to make a good show of running away before ultimately letting them catch up to her. As much as she would have rather been inside hanging out with her sister, she tried to keep the fun going for the little ones. By the time everyone made it back to base, she was genuinely winded.

After the second round of tag, Sofia sat them in a circle under the tree and tried to think of games that would require less athleticism on her part. She could tell that the toddlers in the group were getting sleepy, but, if the noise coming from the house was any indication, their parents weren't likely to take them home any time soon.

Sofia decided to fall back to Xiomara's usual tactic—nothing settled a group of kids with overactive imaginations quite like story time. She arranged her little cousins into a loose semi-circle on the grass and settled in front of them.

"Okay, chamacos, who wants to hear the story of La Llorona?" Sofia grinned when she saw twenty hands shoot up into the air. Sure, she might be hearing complaints from the Tías until New Year's for giving their kids nightmares, but it was tradition. Sofia slept with the lights on for a month after Xiomara told her about the chupacabra, but she liked to think it built character.

"Hundreds of years ago," Sofia began, speaking in a low voice so that the children would have to sit very still and lean in to hear her, "back when Brownsville and Matamoros were just two little villages on either side of the Río Grande, there was a woman named Maria—"

"Like my mom!" Isabella interrupted her, speaking with alarm.

"Yes, like your mom, but this was a different lady," Sofia explained patiently. "Maria was married to a man with the name Cortez, a conquistador."

"What's a conquistador?" asked Michelle, fidgeting in her spot.

Sofia considered, briefly, explaining the intricacies of Spanish colonialism to her six-year-old cousin, but ultimately decided to give her the abridged version.

"He was a rich but very selfish man. And he probably had a horse," Sofia said sagely.

"Ah, bueno." Michelle motioned for her to continue.

"The two of them lived together happily for a time, and she even bore him two children. But, years after marrying Maria, the man left her. Maria was *heartbroken*. She stopped eating. She ripped up all her clothes. She went down to the port every day to see if her husband had returned to her, but he never did." Sofia paused for dramatic effect, staring off into the distance, "One day, mad with grief and hunger, Maria came up with a plot to get her husband's attention. She took their little boys down to the Rio Grande, the very river that most of you crossed today to get to Brownsville, and she *drowned them...*" Sofia whispered sinisterly. She was about to continue when Diego stood up abruptly.

"Ya, stop it. Let's do something else," he whined.

"What, are you scared? Sit down." Sofia snapped.

"I just think the story is boring. I don't want to listen anymore."

Sofia considered her younger cousin. She was tired of him giving her a hard time and knew that she could get him to fall in line with a simple dig at his masculinity. His little sisters were sitting in the front row for their macabre story time, after all. It's what Xiomara or any of the other older cousins might have done. The big kids told scary stories, the little ones slept with nightlights for a couple of weeks and lived to carry on the tradition. It was how they always did things. If anything, as a boy, Diego should be more willing to put on a brave face.

But, as Sofia considered how he may not want to think about ghost children in the river below him as his parents drove him back to Matamoros, she amended that maybe there were some traditions their family could do without.

"Okay, okay, we can do something else. If you guys really want to hear it, I'll finish the story after we sing La Letanía," she said to the rest of the little ones, who had already begun to protest. Sofia reached out a hand and let Diego haul her to her feet, "We'll play tag again, but you're "it" this time."

. . .

Celia Mendoza de Gonzalez really thought she would be better at this by now.

She had started hosting the Posada, taking over for Esperanza, soon after Xiomara was born. She had nearly two decades of experience coordinating this event, and she still felt like she just barely

scraped by every time. Celia would swear on her deathbed that it was

planning the Posada every year that made her start graying in her early

twenties. Regardless of how much time she spent planning and

agonizing, something always, inevitably, went wrong. Either the food

ran out or the speakers wouldn't turn on or, like this year, the branch

of the family that lived in Monterrey couldn't make the drive up.

The logical side of Celia understood the situation. The cartel

activity wasn't nearly as bad as when her daughters were in elementary

school, but some years were better than others. It just so happened

that this year the highway was particularly dangerous. It didn't make

sense for Hector, her younger brother, and his wife Gabby to risk

making the four-hour drive through northern Mexico. Not with their

three sons to think about.

The emotional side of Celia was devastated. If nothing else, the

Posada was supposed to ensure that everyone got to see each other at

least once a year. Their family might be absurdly large and spread out

across two countries, but this night was supposed to bring them

together. It wasn't right and it wasn't fair—that she put all of the work in and there would still be five faces missing from the group photo at the end of the night.

The worst part of Celia, the part that hadn't eaten all day, was also upset to be missing out on Gabby's tres leches cake.

Celia had just about gotten over the situation when her cousin Adrianna came into the kitchen to inform her of yet another pressing situation. It was time for La Letanía, and they didn't have a Joseph.

Though guests usually arrived at the Posada most excited about the food, La Letanía was the main event. That was when all the children dressed up as figures from the nativity scene: Mary, Joseph, shepherds, and angels. There was even a little sheep costume for the youngest Mendoza. The children would knock on the front door of the house, reenacting the scene from the bible where Mary and Joseph searched for a place at the inn. Half of the adults followed behind them with candles, while the other half responded from inside the house. Together, everyone helped the children sing La Letanía Para Pedir Posada.

Celia had made sure that everything was in order. Rocio and Romeo brought the costumes, she had shoved dozens of white candles through plastic cups to keep the wax from dripping on people's fingers, and the song lyrics were printed on over a hundred sheets of paper—more than enough to go around. And still, not a single one of the boys in the family wanted to play Joseph.

She appealed to the boys directly, at first. Celia found most of her young nephews outside, chasing each other around with firecrackers. She stopped Lucas in his tracks, placing both hands on his shoulders, and knelt to meet him at eye level. "Lucas, querido, can you do me a big favor, please? I need you to put on a costume and be Joseph for the Letanía this year. Could you do that for me?" Celia smiled warmly at him.

"No thanks! We're pretty busy." Lucas dashed off before Celia could get another word in. She turned to her older nephews, Allan and Diego, but both followed after him, throwing snappers at each other's feet.

Celia trudged back to the kitchen to regroup. She took her case to the boys' mothers, but she could not convince a single one of them to force their kid into the Joseph costume.

"Son niños, Celia, what do you expect? You want them to sit pretty for pictures? Just be happy they're playing outside and not tearing up your fancy sitting room," Adrianna said dismissively. Celia's eyelid twitched, but she didn't respond in anger. Instead, she picked up Adrianna's sweating beer bottle and placed it on the coaster that her cousin had absentmindedly ignored.

Feeling defeated and attacked on all sides, Celia found comfort in locking herself in the pantry, where she could seethe in private. She listened to the Christmas music that seeped through the closed door and glared at a bag of rice. There she was, once again bending over backward to make sure that this party happened, and none of the malagradecidos in her family could deign to help her with La Lentania. God forbid a ten-year-old boy be forced to put on a costume and sing with the family that raised him.

Celia heard the click of the pantry door and turned to see that her husband, Eduardo, had joined her.

"Que onda?" he asked.

"Ya," Celia said, "I'm done. I'm never hosting this party again. Please never let me do this again." Celia hunched forward and leaned her head on Eduardo's shoulder. He rubbed slow circles on her back.

"It's okay, amor, it'll be okay," he reassured her.

"I don't know why I do this to myself! I never even enjoy these damn parties, I'm always so stressed. And now we're not even gonna do La Letanía." Celia sniffed. "What was even the point."

"The point was that you love your family," Eduardo reminded her with a smile, even though she couldn't see it, "you do it because you know how important it is for everyone to get together. You saw Sofia chasing her cousins through the yard, right? And Xo drinking champurrado with her Tita and her Tío Santiago? Those things only get to happen once a year, and it's because of you."

"Still," said Celia, still speaking into her hands, "no one ever appreciates it. Not enough to put on the stupid costume."

Eduardo tucked Celia's hair behind her ear and leaned down to kiss his wife's temple, "About that... I think I have an idea."

. . .

Esperanza Mendoza watched La Letanía from the middle of the crowd. She didn't have a role to play, so she got to take her time drinking in the scene. Celia and Eduardo laughed through their lines as Mary and Joseph. The costumes weren't even close to fitting them, but they still hung them around their necks like ponchos, just to get the idea across. Sofia walked with little Michelle, dressed in the tiny sheep costume, propped up against her hip. Xiomara could be seen through the kitchen window, serving hot mugs of champurrado for everyone to share once they got back inside and needed to warm up from the chilly December night.

Esperanza smiled at her sprawling family. Bien encimosos, the lot of them. But it was the night of the Posada, and all was well.

WINTER TEXANS PART I

South Padre Island, Texas

2015

Paulina Jones walked with four fish bones in her right pocket and two seashells in her left. She had tucked a sand dollar into the waistband of her shorts, and it pressed against her stomach every time she reached down.

It was a bright December morning, and Paulina squinted through the sun's glare as it bounced off the gulf and into her eyes. She had been beach combing since dawn and was sorely disappointed in her current wares. It didn't help that she only took the best of the ocean's flotsam. The bones and shells went into the mason jar that sat on her nightstand that she'd been filling for the better part of two years and she was saving any bits of sea glass, coral, and driftwood for a sculpture she had designed. Not on paper, not yet, but she thought about it every night before she went to sleep.

She was so focused on her projects and scanning the packed brown sand that she didn't notice the other girl on the beach until she almost tripped over her.

"Chingadamadre," Paulina swore, the curse slipping a little too naturally from her ten-year-old mouth. "Why are you just sitting there?"

In her carelessness, Paulina had trampled right over the girl's sandcastle. It looked like it might have been beautiful, just a moment before. Two multi-story castles, connected by a shell-encrusted bridge and surrounded by a narrow moat.

"Oh, sorry," said Paulina. The other girl seemed to be about her age, and was close to tears, but she wasn't looking at the castle. Instead, she stared silently at the sea. Paulina followed her gaze and could just barely make out a pale pink pail bobbing out there in the waves, maybe twenty meters out.

"Is that yours?" she asked. The other girl nodded vigorously. "Aren't you gonna go get it?" The girl bit her lip, glanced back at the tall flagpole mounted near the beach access, and shook her head. A red flag snapped against the wind, warning of high tides and a strong undertow.

Paulina pursed her lips, considering, before she started digging treasures out of her pockets and offering them to the unknown girl. "Here, take these. Don't lose 'em, they're important," she warned, before marching into the ocean.

The cold bit into her as the first wave swept over her feet and up to her mid-calf. It was 78 degrees outside, typical of a South Texas winter, but the ocean was unforgiving. She lost her breath, though not her resolve, as she waded in deeper. She started treading water once the ocean floor dropped out from under her and transitioned into a steady breaststroke. Paulina bobbed up and down with each wave, seemingly making no progress at all, until she reached the second sandbar, where the pail had been caught by the lower tide and floated in lazy circles.

Her limbs were numb by the time she emerged back on the shore, where the other girl held out her beach towel—sandy, but dry. Paulina traded her for the pail, "Ahí estas," she said.

"Thank you," the girl finally spoke, her eyebrows knit together. Her voice was high and clear.

"Don't worry about it. So, not much of a swimmer?" Paulina asked as she dried herself off. She held out her hand for the shells and bones she had given the girl for safekeeping. "My name's Paulina, what's yours?"

"Rosemary," she responded, looking down at her feet, "and I *can* swim… I just—I shouldn't."

"Uh, why?" asked Paulina. Having grown up on the Gulf Coast, she had been swimming in the open ocean since she was old enough to toddle.

Rosemary jerked her chin over toward the flagpole, where Paulina spied a typical beach-day setup—a big umbrella and an old man dozing in a fold-out chair, a paperback book open face-down on his lap with a picture of a bird on the cover. The man wore a visor, sunglasses, and a navy blue sun shirt. "See that guy over there? He's my grandpa. I'm not allowed to get into the water without him, but I was too scared to wake him up. He's not mean, but just kind of… cranky," Rosemary said, wrinkling her nose.

"Ah." Paulina nodded knowingly. "I get that, but at least you didn't break any rules. Why don't we rebuild your castle? Then it'll be like none of this even happened."

Rosemary nodded, smiling, and the girls sat down on either side of the twin castles. As they were talking, Paulina had peeked into the mesh beach bag that sat open next to Rosemary. In it, there was a multitude of beach toys, most of them still in their packaging. Bright red shovels, so unlike the ones that Paulina used—which were discolored and made brittle by UV rays. Plastic molds in the shapes of starfish and sharks that could be filled with wet sand and used to decorate the bottom of the moat. And, best of all, a set of flags in every color of the rainbow that could dress up even the most run-down of sandcastles.

Paulina waited until Rosemary took the toys out of the bag before reaching over and grabbing a shovel. It made a satisfying crater when she used it to begin carving out a new, deeper moat.

"So, where y'all from?" Paulina asked, as her new friend leveled both sandcastles to start over. Rosemary was incredibly pale, blonde, and spoke in the heavy-voweled English of a real American. No one had to tell Paulina that she wasn't from the Rio Grande Valley. To her credit, Rosemary didn't respond like someone being singled out as an outsider.

"We're from Michigan, actually. I'm usually with my mom and dad, but I spend my breaks with my grandparents. They always come down to Texas around Christmas. It's easier than dealing with the snow. Plus, they like birdwatching."

"That sounds nice," Paulina said politely. Just a couple of weeks before, she had overheard her father complaining about Winter Texans, gringos who came down from the northern states and rented houses and condominiums on South Padre Island during the winter months. Sure, they got the restaurants and souvenir shops through the off-season, but they weren't known for their willingness to assimilate into the local culture. *They come for the weather, se quedan por los mendigos pájaros, and they complain about Mexicans the* entire time *they are here,"* her dad had said.

"What about you?" Rosemary asked, "Is your family from around here?"

"Pos, más o menos. My mom was born in Matamoros, that's the city on the Mexican side of the border. My dad grew up in Brownsville, on this side. Then we moved out here to the island when I was little."

As Paulina spoke, Rosemary's eyes grew wide and she looked up and down the beach.

"Are you out here alone?" she asked, "Where are your parents?"

Paulina stood up and motioned for Rosemary to do the same. She turned her by the shoulders and pointed west. "You see that blue house over there, just past the dunes? That's my parents' place. My mom's keeping an eye on me through the kitchen window while she makes lunch." The lie came easily enough, but Rosemary had a difficult time accepting it.

"But don't they worry about you? Are you okay being out here alone?"

Those are two very different questions, Paulina thought to herself.

"They know I'm a strong swimmer, and I don't go far." The truth of it was that both of her parents had left the house early that morning. Her father for his job at the Valley International Airport, her mother for her shift at Pirates' Landing—a tourist trap restaurant best known for their popcorn shrimp and creepy pirate statues. The house was theirs, that much was true, but there was no one watching her through the window. For lunch, she would eat cold cuts and cheese slices. Maybe a quesadilla, if she bothered with the gas stove.

"If you say so. Let's stick together, though. Here, take this." Rosemary handed her a dark purple sandcastle mold, which Paulina accepted eagerly.

On their third attempt, the girls found the exact consistency of sand that they needed for the castles to come out crisp and with clear details: medium-wet and tightly packed. Rosemary had the idea to dust the inside of the molds with dry sand so that they would slide off smoothly, without tearing off the tips of the pointed towers. She said she learned the trick from her grandmother, a baker. Paulina decorated their new kingdom with shells and flags and, after they finished the moat, she used the pink pail to fill it with seawater.

The girls chatted as they worked. Despite growing up on opposite ends of the country, they agreed on all of the important things. They both liked poodles and constellations and fantasy books that took place in boarding schools. They disliked math homework and black olives and boys who made fun of girls when they liked them. They both wanted to travel the world when they grew up. They both loved the ocean.

It was late afternoon by the time Rosemary's grandfather stirred from his nap and Paulina noticed a change in her new friend. Rosemary stood up straighter, shook the sand out of her hair, and kept glancing at her grandfather as he stretched and rolled his shoulders. She didn't look scared of him, exactly, but she held herself like someone about to be evaluated.

"I should start heading home," Paulina said, getting ready to move on. She thought maybe Rosemary would relax without a witness to whatever encounter she anticipated.

"No, wait, don't go yet." Rosemary reached out and caught Paulina's wrist. "It's too soon. Oh! Do you want to come get lunch with us? I could introduce you to my grandpa and we can ask him. Do you think your mom would mind much?"

Paulina shifted uncomfortably in place. "I don't know about that. She probably wants me home by now." She noticed the jut of Rosemary's lip and felt a twinge of guilt. "But I guess I could give it a try."

"Great!" Rosemary tossed the sandy beach toys into her bag and Paulina glanced back at the old man. He seemed friendly enough, but Paulina had a healthy fear of most adults, especially outsiders.

Once they packed their camp, Rosemary threw her arm around Paulina's waist and walked her over to her grandfather to make her introductions.

"Pops, this is my new friend, Paulina. She helped me make those sandcastles over there." Rosemary brandished her hand proudly. "Paulina, this is my grandfather, Sergeant Robert Thompson."

Paulina gave him a small wave "Hello, sir."

"It's nice to meet you, Paulina," he said. His face was covered in sun spots and his eyes crinkled when he smiled.

"I know we gotta leave for lunch soon, but I was wondering if maybe we could bring her with us, pretty please?" Rosemary grinned widely at her grandfather, but he was looking at Paulina.

His stare was just shy of uncomfortable, but it was enough for Paulina to grow intensely aware of the hole in her cutoff shorts, the ratty state of her hair, and the color of her skin—deeply tanned from hours spent in the South Texas sun.

"And what would Paulina's parents say about us whisking her away without notice?" he asked.

Rosemary nudged Paulina with a bony elbow.

"I would have to ask my mom," Paulina said hesitantly.

Rosemary raised an eyebrow at her.

"So, can she borrow your phone to call her?" Rosemary asked.

Mr. Thompson paused for a moment, "I suppose there's no harm in that." He reached into his pocket and handed his phone to Paulina. "Do you know your mom's phone number, sweetheart?"

"I do, thank you." Paulina walked a few paces away to make the call. She dialed quickly and grew more anxious with each ring, unsure of what outcome she hoped for.

On the fifth ring, her mom picked up, "Mande? Who is this?"

"Hi Amá, it's me—Polly. I gotta ask you something real quick."

"What is it? I'm at work, it's the lunch rush."

"Well I made this friend while I was at the beach today and now her family wants to take me out to lunch. Is that okay?"

"What kind of family? Do we know these people?"

"They're tourists—gringos, but friendly."

"Bueno, I guess that's fine. Just make sure you're home before your dad is."

"Great! Ahí te veó! Bye." She hung up quickly and turned on her heel to head back towards Rosemary and her grandfather, but stopped short. Though they argued in hushed tones, the sea breeze carried their voices back to Paulina.

"What's the problem? She's my friend," Rosemary said sharply.

"Well, honey, you just met the girl. We don't know who she is or where she's from..."

"She's from here, her family is from here."

"*Exactly,* I just think you need to ask a couple more questions before inviting someone along. Besides, our reservations at the Palm Lounge are just for us and your grandma, we don't even know if they'll let us add—" he stopped talking when Paulina walked over.

Paulina kept her tone even and held his gaze while she said, "I'm so sorry, my mom really wants me to come home for lunch, she spent *all* afternoon making paella de mariscos, but thank you *so* much for the invitation," she said sweetly.

"Well, that's too bad," said Mr. Thompson, as she returned his cellphone.

"Oh," was all that Rosemary said as she looked at the ground and dug her feet into the sand.

"I'll start packing up the car so you girls can say your goodbyes," Mr. Thompson offered diplomatically. He plucked the heavy beach bag off of Rosemary's shoulder, where the straps had left deep red grooves on her freckled skin.

"I'm sorry for the trouble," Rosemary said quietly, as she watched her grandfather walk away, down the path that led to the parking lot, "I just—I liked talking to you. I don't any have friends here, just my grandparents. I didn't want it to be over yet."

Paulina sighed, "Don't worry about it. I get the feeling."

"So, what now?"

"Well, now I have to go home and you have to go with your grandpa, but let's keep in touch, yeah? Use the number, call me, we'll figure it out."

Before she set off for home, Paulina pressed a gift into Rosemary's hand. It was the sea dollar—long dead, but still beautiful. It was the only one that Paulina had found in a year of beach combing.

"Just in case you don't come back." She pulled Rosemary in for a hug. "But please, come back," she whispered.

YO LO VI

Matamoros, Tamaulipas

1995

I was eighteen years old and about to leave home for the first time when my father finally told me about the murders, though I was just a kid when they happened. I was, what, twelve then? All I remember from that spring was when El Rol stopped—and how it never really started up again. In this town, with nothin' else going on, it's gotta get pretty bad pa que no haya nadie en la calle.

El Rol was everything in Matamoros back in the 80s. Every evening during the long days of spring and summer, teenagers would pile into their cars and drive real slow up and down the town's main street, Avenida Álvaro Obregón. Windows rolled down, music blasting. Sometimes people waved down their buddies in other cars and pulled over to the side of the road to kick back then and there— drinking cold cheves in the back of their pickup trucks as though the cops couldn't show up any second. Most of us drove used cars, then. Real clunkers. It wasn't like it is now, with all the new-money narco kids driving their souped-up BMWs. Anyone with a nice car had to put hours into restoring whatever vintage thing his dad or tío had sitting on cinder blocks in the front yard. It took work.

I didn't have my own car, of course, but I had a cousin with a convertible Mercedes and a bad smoking habit. Benny was always easy to bribe. All it took was half a carton of cigarettes and he was driving me and my friends from the Río Bravo all the way downtown. Benny wasn't a total impertinente, though. I mean, we were still pretty young and he always made sure to drop us back home before 9 pm at the latest. During the day, El Rol was for anybody—from middle schoolers hanging with their kinda-responsible cousins to the Catholic school girls from Villa Maria. After dark, though, it was a different crowd that stuck around. Older, meaner, more likely to start fights at the cantinas… My dad would have killed Benny if he let us fall in with that group.

Unfortunately for me, I only got to enjoy a few weeks of cruising along Obregón before the town mandated a curfew that shut down El Rol. I didn't know much about it at the time, but the authorities were all losing their minds because of some missing college student. Desaparecidos weren't unheard of in our part of Mexico, people went missing all the time with all the illegal shit going back and forth over the border, but this kid wasn't local. He was from the other side—a spring breaker from Texas who had crossed into Matamoros with his buddies for a bit of drinking.

The story made the news a couple of times, but I wasn't thinking about it much. I was more concerned with soccer tryouts and getting my hands on Benny's car keys—I had other things going on. To be honest, it didn't really cross my mind again after that spring break.

At least, until I was getting ready to move to Monterrey, and I decided to pick a fight over that damn amulet.

My father was always the superstitious type. By day, he was just a supervisor at one of the maquiladoras by the river. After hours, though, he served as the neighborhood curandero. It wasn't anything too crazy—he didn't do spells or nothin'—but he helped people out with his little herbs and blessings and whatever. There was always some tea to drink or a saint to pray to. Lots of blessings with talismans and holy water. It was all shit my abuelita taught him—folksy medicine that people practiced in the countryside, where there weren't any real hospitals and the TVs didn't pick up anything good.

I was packing my stuff, preparing for my big move as a university student at El Technológical de Monterrey, when I noticed a cardboard box on my bed. It was filled to the brim with my father's curandero supplies. Glass bottles of holy water, candles, un ojo de venado, bunches of herbs wrapped in twine—cenizo, yerba buena, others that I didn't recognize. Sitting next to it was this big gold amulet. It was about the size of my open palm and depicted an angel holding a sword and chain over the devil—who he crushed underfoot. The detail on it was insane, but the whole thing kinda freaked me out. My dad had scrawled a note on the top left corner of the box: *"para tu protección."*

"No mames güey," I muttered to myself, scooping the package up and taking it with me into the kitchen, where my dad drank his morning coffee. I placed the box on the table and held the amulet out in front of his face. He looked at it, then at me, but didn't reach out and take it.

"¿Que onda contigo?" he asked.

"¿Pa que me das todo esto? I'm going to Monterrey, not the afterlife. I don't need all of this. Thanks, pero no thanks." I put the amulet down on the kitchen table and slid it over to him.

"Hijo, what's the harm? I'm just trying to keep you safe." He ran his hand over his beard, massaging his jaw.

"Yeah, yeah, I know. But it's not like all of this voodoo brujo stuff actually works."

My father raised his eyebrows at me, forehead creasing. "Really? None of it? I'll be sure to let my clients know that they're wasting their time with my 'voodoo brujo stuff.'"

I crossed my arms. "You know what I mean. It's fine here, where people believe in it. Pero over there in the city?" I let out a low whistle. "This is some puro Indio shit."

"Bájale, Humberto. There's no reason to be disrespectful," he said, giving me a stern look. He finished his coffee and held out the mug. "Here, pour me another. And get some for yourself, too. We should talk about this."

I did what he asked, grabbing another mug from the cabinet over the sink and filling both with the last of the coffee from the pot. It was dark as all hell, almost sludgy, but I figured it would be enough to get me through what would probably be a long conversation about faith and tradition y 'las cosas que importan.'

My dad had his eyes closed when I got back to the table, but he opened them when he heard my chair scrape against the tiled floor of our kitchen.

"Here," I said and placed the mug in front of him. He wrapped both of his calloused hands around it, warming them. We sat quietly for a few moments and I listened to the tick of the kitchen clock as I waited for him to speak again.

"Bueno, let me get this straight: all of these things that we do, you don't believe any of it?" he asked. "The rituals, the remedies, the jumping over a flame to keep your soul in place, none of it? Ever?"

"Pos, maybe when I was little. And I don't mind it now, really. It probably does something, like, psychologically, pero no I don't think curandismo *actually* works."

My dad mulled over my answer before responding, "Yeah, I used to think like that too, before. Even when I did the rituals, I never knew whether or not they were working. I just went through the motions."

"What changed?" I asked. Thinking back on my childhood, so thoroughly steeped in superstition, I couldn't remember a time before my father believed wholeheartedly in the work he did.

"Cambió cuando lo vi. I saw the devil, once. He was made out of smoke." My father took a long sip of his coffee. "Humberto, what do you remember about the murder of Mark Kilroy?

The question caught me off-guard—it had been years since I last heard the name, not since I was twelve years old and sitting in the back of Benny's Mercedes, breathing in the scent of cigarette smoke and hot asphalt. After the missing person's case was resolved and Matamoros got off the national news, it was the last thing anyone in this town wanted to talk about. The whole thing blew over before I found it in myself to care.

I scratched the back of my head. "Pos, nothing specific. I don't get into it with all the narco stuff, and I think that's when it was just starting up. I remember when he went missing, I remember there were rumors for a while that Sara Aldrete had something to do with it. You know, Alex's cousin?"

"Narco stuff." My dad exhaled deeply. "It was more than just narco stuff, hijo. And yes, Sara did find herself in the middle of it. La Bruja de Matamoros, they called her. La Madrina. But it wasn't her that started it. Ese pinche Cubano corrupted her. Do you know the name Adolfo de Jesus Constanzo?"

"No." I took a sip of my coffee and realized it was much colder than I expected it to be.

"He was a Cuban national. A sadomasochist. He came to Matamoros and brought Santería with him. All of the worst stuff of that damned religion—animal sacrifice, blood rituals. By the time that group started digging up graves en el cementerio, Constanzo had half of the Matamoros police department in his pocket. He'd convinced everyone that his rituals could protect them—empower them. Narcos, cops, politicians—he was in with all of them."

"Y que? He and Sara are the ones that killed Mark Kilroy? You're telling me that was some kind of sacrifice?" I swallowed hard, thinking of Alex, Sara's younger cousin. We were altar boys together, back in elementary school. He was an interesting kid—always picking up bugs and little animals during recess. Once, a lizard crawled out of his pocket in the middle of the homily and I had to help him catch it before the priest noticed.

"The two of them killed more people than just Kilroy. There were over a dozen bodies in the ground by the time we found them." My father sat back in his chair, waiting to see my reaction.

I felt my pulse at my neck. "I didn't know you were involved," I said slowly.

"I didn't want to be," he responded. "It was late March when that kid went missing, during the last round of the usual spring break desmadre. Yeah, I thought it was odd. You know how the cholos around here are about messing with gringos—it gets too messy when the American government gets involved. I remember thinking he would turn up on a beach somewhere, hungover but fine, but then on April 11th, 1989—I'll never forget that cursed day—I got a call from your Tío Mando. You remember Mando?"

"Yeah, sure."

"Well, he was on the force then, and he called me. A bunch of them, a mix of Matamoros police and U.S. federal agents, turned up at Santa Elena Ranch on a tip. It was a slice of land owned by one of the drug lords that employed Constanzo. Nothing too fancy, but near the river—easy to move stuff out of. Anyway, once the cops showed up they got real suspicious real quick. There were bones all over the ground, animal heads, scraps of bloody fabric… awful, awful things. Once they got inside the ranch house, they started to see what was really going on. The gringos, they didn't get it—they wanted to start taking pictures and collecting evidence right away. But Chief Ayala, he saw the signs."

My father paused his story, staring into my face as though searching for some kind of recognition. I looked around the room instead of responding—noticing, for the first time, a crack that spiderwebbed on the corner of the kitchen wall and how the white paint, yellowed by generations of chain smokers, chipped away from it.

My father continued his story.

"Inside the house, there were empty liquor bottles on the floor… symbols carved into the banisters… and, in the center of the room, an iron cauldron. Constanzo's followers—the ones he left behind—called it a nganga. When Ayala looked inside, he saw that it was filled with blood and bone. He knew that they had entered the house of the devil."

My father stopped for a moment and began unpacking the box of supplies in front of him. He pulled out a black candle, a matchbook, an ojo de venado charm, and a plastic bag filled with dried eggshells.

"Hijo, tráeme el molcajete and the sea salt," he asked. Slowly, I got up and brought him the mortar and pestle and dish of salt from where we kept them, next to the stove. He used the molcajete to grind down the eggshells and salt as he continued his story.

"Ayala gave the order to halt the investigation until they could get a curandero to come in and bless the grounds," he said. "That was me. It was the middle of a workday, but I took an early lunch. No tenía la menor idea what I was getting myself into. I was just a yerbero at the time. I knew what teas could soothe pain, which herbs could cure an upset stomach. I knew to put garlic on insect bites… I didn't know the first thing about banishing evil. But I took all of the holy water I could find, and I hoped it would be enough."

"I don't—I don't remember any of this…" I struggled to get the words out as I tried to imagine my father, who had only ever been taught how to heal, walking into a scene of the occult. I imagined the smell of it—the hot air rolling off the slow-moving river, the rotting animal carcasses and greasy bones, the sulfur… wasn't the devil meant to smell like rotten eggs?

"Hijo, I didn't want you to. I didn't want to remember it myself. When I got there, everyone was expecting some kind of shaman show, but I didn't even know where to begin. As soon as I stepped out of the car, I could feel the evil washing over me like a sickness. Like something that wanted to infect me. But I had this with me." He tapped on the gold amulet on the table in front of him to punctuate his words. "San Miguel Arcángel, the protector against evil. I drew strength from it, and let it shield me. I used the water to cleanse everything I saw—starting from the edge of the ranch and making my way towards the house. But then I saw…" His voice grew quieter. "I saw… a pair of little white tennis shoes… bloodied, dirty, meant for a child, sitting next to a pile of trash."

"Apá, stop. You don't have to—"

"I thought of you, mijo, waiting for me back home. And the prayers started coming from somewhere different. Somewhere truer." As my father spoke, his voice thick with emotion, he pulled out a pocket knife and used it to carve a hole into the black candle.

"What did they do when you finished the ritual?" I asked, watching his hands as he pressed the ojo de venado charm into the hollow that he had created in the candle. He cleaned the wax residue off his knife with the cuff of his sleeve.

"They started digging up bodies. I wanted to leave, but Mando asked me to stay. To watch over them. They had the nephew of one of the drug lords pointing out the unmarked graves. Bien pendejo, but he went along with it because he thought the mark of the devil protected him. Se arrepintío bien gacho when they put a gun to his back and had him digging up bodies 'til the sun went down. When every grave turned up another Mexican, the feds started getting real testy—asking him where Kilroy was. He finally led them to a spot a few meters away from the rest of the graves. A place marked by a metal wire sticking out of the ground."

"What was the wire for?" I leaned forward in my chair.

"Permíteme," he said, and took a moment to finish assembling whatever altar he was so intent on creating. He used the hilt of his knife to flatten out the mound of salt and eggshells and created a well in the center, where he placed the black candle. He lit it with a match and I wrinkled my nose as the smell of sulfur filled the room.

"Andalé, just tell me," I urged.

My father gave me a long look before responding. "The devil-worshippers had woven a wire through Mark Kilroy's spinal column, so that they could pull it out of the ground when his body decomposed. Later, I learned that Constanzo wanted to make a necklace out of it."

"Fuckin' hell…" I said, feeling bile creep up my throat. The candlelight made shadows dance across my father's face. His eyes looked black, deeply set, and so, so old.

"Hijo, I felt for the kid. I really did. The TV, the American cops, the reporters, they all made sure of it. I know more details about his life than half the vatos I went to school with. He wanted to be a doctor, he played basketball in college, he loved his mom—he was a person, just like the rest of us. The other thirteen bodies we found that day, though, they were people too. But their names never made the news, they were just that—bodies. But one of them, one of them was my friend."

"Who was it?" I asked.

"Saul, my neighbor when I was growing up. Good kid, un poco raro, but harmless. One time, your Tío Santiago and I got invited out to his family's ranch to hunt boar. Instead, we spent the whole weekend shooting firecrackers at each other and stealing beers out of his papí's cooler. We didn't stay close, but I knew him well enough to identify his body."

"Apá, I am so, so sorry. I didn't know—"

"Save it, there's still more."

"What happened next?"

"Nothing, for a time. They caught some of the lower-level cult members that day, the news started referring to them as the 'satanic narcos' of Matamoros, but Constanzo and Sara had already left town. For weeks, no one knew where they were or if they would be able to find them. I wanted to stay out of it after that terrible day at Santa Elena, but Mando kept me updated. He was the one who told me when Sheriff Gavito over there in Brownsville wanted to look into 'alternative solutions.' He wanted to know if there was something I could do to draw Constanzo out—curandismo contra santería."

"What did you tell him?"

"I told him we needed to burn the whole ranch to the ground," my father said solemnly, with that same faraway look in his eyes as before. In his irises, I could just barely make out the flickering flame of the black candle.

"But how were they going to connect Constanzo and Sara to the murders if you burned it all down?"

"Hijo, we already knew they were guilty. Everyone knew. We just had to find them. And I would have done *anything* to drive that evil out of this town. To keep you safe. And when we set fire to

Constanzo's nganga, burning the rest of the house down with it, yo lo vi. Créeme que yo lo vi. I saw the moment that the devil left that house, I saw him in the smoke." My father reached out from across the table and took my hands in his. "Mijo, I have learned that there are some things that holy water cannot cleanse. In this life, there are things that we must give to the flames."

"And it worked?"

He nodded. "They found Constanzo in Mexico City within a day. Sara betrayed him, and he was shot dead by one of his own men. They were nothing without his power, and he lost it the moment that we destroyed his nganga. Now all we have are the ashes, and the stories to pass on."

"And that's why you're telling me this? To scare me into believing?" I started to pull away, but he let go first. My father took the amulet and placed it in my open hand. He curled my fingers around it and squeezed.

"I will only ever try to protect you, Humberto," my father said, "What you want to believe is up to you." He blew out the candle and left, taking both of our mugs with him to the kitchen sink.

I stared at the smoke as it curled and rose and disappeared to nothing. I thought of my father—of the evil he saw that day and the darkness he wanted so badly to protect me from. I twisted the gold chain around my fingers, still warm from his touch. Before I got up from the table, I put the amulet around my neck, and I made the sign of the cross

Winter Texans Part II

South Padre Island, Texas

2018

The drive to the Shores was a hot one—even in December, even with the windows rolled all the way down. Paulina used her left hand to hold her hair in place at the nape of her neck in a vain attempt at preventing it from whipping around in the wind. She stuck her right hand out of the car window, feeling the breeze slip between her fingertips as she stared out to the coast. The northern end of South Padre was the only part of the island that was still mostly untouched. No souvenir shops or restaurants stood to disrupt the pristine view—it was just miles and miles of softly cresting sand dunes and the teal sea.

It was three years after the encounter on the beach, and Paulina's mom was driving her out to Rosemary's grandparents' house. They rented a place out at the Shores, a private neighborhood on the north side of the island. It hadn't been easy to convince Paulina's mom to make the drive. Paulina had to promise to clean out the gutters without complaint and, in the end, it was mostly her mother's curiosity over what the wealthiest neighborhood on the island looked like that motivated her.

Paulina thought this might be a bonding moment for the two of them, she wanted to tell her mom all about Rosemary and why she was so excited to see her again. Instead, her mom used the opportunity to complain about the tourists. Paulina tried to tune her out, but it was hard to ignore.

"… I had this one lady who came into the restaurant, quejandose bien gacho porque she couldn't find 'any good queso' this far south. Not queso flameado, mind you, she meant 'kayyyso.' How the gringos say it. You know, the liquid cheese stuff? Que pena." Paulina's mom laughed without humor.

"I'm sure the Thompsons aren't like that," Paulina said, looking out the window to the ocean. The waves were dark gray under an overcast sky. "Rosemary wouldn't complain about that kind of thing. She loves trying new stuff."

Paulina's mother arched an eyebrow. "No me digas."

They were silent until they pulled up to the address, when Paulina's mom let out a low whistle.

The house was three stories tall, bright white, and had a wrap-around porch. Paulina broke out in a sweat when she saw it, but got out of the car without hesitation. She could feel her pulse thrumming in her neck, but her desire to see Rosemary outweighed her apprehension. As she turned around to wave goodbye, she saw that her mom was already backing out of the driveway. She hadn't even waited until Paulina got to the door.

Paulina hadn't seen Rosemary since the day they met. The two years following their chance encounter, Paulina spent her winter break with her cousins in Valle Hermoso. Last year, Rosemary's grandparents had splurged on a trip to Hawaii in lieu of their usual migration down to the Rio Grande Valley. Though the girls were teenagers now, they had maintained the friendship of their youth. They messaged each other often and talked on the phone at least once a week. They even ran a joint fan account for their favorite band. Paulina had a difficult time finding a group when she got to middle school, mostly due to her niche interests and preference for solitude, but she valued her friendship with Rosemary.

Rosemary, who stayed on the phone with her until dawn when she had yet another world-ending fight with her mother. Rosemary, who let her ramble on and on about tide patterns and shell morphology. Rosemary, who confided in her when no one else did.

Slowly, Paulina inched up the driveway, her sneakers scuffing along the pavement with every step.

The anticipation made Paulina's stomach churn. If she made a good impression, she could spend the next three weeks hanging out with her closest friend, showing her the best parts of the island, the parts that Winter Texans rarely stuck around to see. They could climb the jetties at Isla Blanca, attend Friday-night movie screenings at the lighthouse, and go crab hunting by night. If it didn't go well, though, if Rosemary's family didn't warm up to her… well, it didn't bear thinking. At the very least, Paulina would have to make a new Tumblr account.

Paulina climbed up the porch steps but stopped short of the front door. She smoothed her hands over her sundress—her best one, her only one. She figured she shouldn't show up to lunch wearing her usual cutoff shorts and tank top. In a moment of impulse the night before, Paulina chopped off the bottom three inches of her hair, which she had dyed bright red using Cherry Kool-Aid. Her copper-brown hair stopped a few inches above her shoulders now, feeling unnaturally light. She was about to reach out and knock on the door when it swung open.

"You're early, perfect!" Rosemary pulled her into a hug before she could acknowledge the non-greeting.

"Happy to see you too." Paulina's voice was muffled by Rosemary's sweater-clad shoulder. They had been the same height when they were younger, but Rosemary's recent growth spurt left her half a head taller than Paulina. She had braces now, too, and the rubber bands on them made her grin flash pink.

Rosemary pulled back and Paulina noticed the sprinkle of acne on her chin, "I just can't believe you're here," said Rosemary, "I mean, I know you live here, but now you're *here* here. Outside of my computer screen and everything."

"I know what you mean, you barely look real." She reached over and pushed Rosemary's shoulder, checking.

"Okay, okay, let's get you inside. Nana is dying to meet you."

As Rosemary led her past the foyer and into the living room, Paulina tried to keep from staring a more-than-normal amount. Though she had lived on South Padre Island her whole life, she had never had any reason to come to the Shores, much less step inside one of the massive houses. The inside of the house was bright and airy, all of the windows were open and the sheer linen curtains that covered them rustled with the breeze. The ceilings were impossibly high, and a grand staircase with a carved wooden banister led to the upper stories.

The house was tidy, but not suffocatingly so. Paulina spotted a half-finished puzzle on the coffee table, two tennis rackets leaning against the fireplace, and a pair of binoculars sitting on a windowsill. And books. Books everywhere. Literary classics, books on economics, and mass-market paperback murder mysteries they must have bought while waiting in line at Blue Marlin, the island's only supermarket. Paulina breathed in deeply, the room smelled like cinnamon and sea salt. She tried to commit the scene to memory, unsure if she would get another peak behind the curtain of wealth that separated her from the island's seasonal residents.

She thought of her own house, just ten miles south. She thought of its peeling blue paint, irreparably damaged from the constant buffeting of wind, sand, and salt. It was usually clean, but mostly from lack of use. Most days, it looked like no one lived there at all. It was just a way station for her parents to rest in between long shifts. The only room with any personality was Paulina's, where she existed in solitude and surrounded herself with small treasures.

Rosemary led Paulina through the whole first story of the house and out the back porch. If she didn't feel the need to acknowledge that her family lived in a literal mansion through the winter, Paulina certainly was not going to.

They found Rosemary's grandparents setting the table outside. It was a perfect winter day, 75 degrees and cloudless. They both turned when the sliding glass door clicked shut behind the girls. For a moment, they didn't say anything, and Paulina felt her stomach flip.

"Hi there!" she said with a drawl. "Thank you so much for inviting me over for lunch, you're too kind. And your home is so lovely." She realized too late that she was leaning hard on the Southern charm.

Rosemary's grandmother walked around the table and greeted her with a warm hug. "Well, aren't you sweet? The pleasure is ours, we're so excited to finally meet Rosie's little friend. We've heard a *lot* about you."

"Good things, I hope." Paulina smiled, trying to maintain her composure as Rosemary's grandfather walked over. In the years following their introduction, Paulina had spent some time debating what she may have done differently, if there had been any other possible outcome to the situation. He hadn't been *that* awful to her, all things considered. Telling his granddaughter to be wary of strangers wasn't the same as calling her a slur, but she could only assume that his apprehension was limited to Mexican-looking beach rats. The neighborhood kids at the Shores were probably pre-screened by their tax brackets.

"Remind me of your name, dear," he said, holding out his hand.

"Paulina," she said meekly, then cleared her throat and tried again, "Paulina Jones, sir. It's great to see you again…" She reached out and shook his hand.

"You can call me Mr. Thompson."

"Mr. Thompson, sir." Paulina winced, hoping to God it didn't sound like she was mocking him and his military background. Mrs. Thompson rolled her eyes next to him, though.

"Well, you can call me Nana. And don't even try with all that 'yes, ma'am' nonsense." Mrs. Thompson led her to the table by the elbow. "Now why don't we go ahead and start eating?"

Lunch was a simple affair. Cream cheese and cucumber sandwiches, a harvest bowl salad with blackened chicken, and a freshly squeezed lemonade to wash it down. Paulina could scarcely taste any of it. The introductions had gone well enough, but she still felt distinctly out of her element. She stayed quiet for the first half of the meal, while Rosemary and her grandfather discussed a book on WWII that they had both read recently. Once that petered out, though, Mrs. Thompson turned to Paulina.

"So, your family name is Jones, is it? We haven't met too many people with that sort of last name since coming here. Are you folks from around here?"

Paulina hastily swallowed a bite of chicken. "We're from the area, yes. My mom's family is from Matamoros, but she's been living on this side for a while. Since about when I was born."

"And your father, he's from here as well?"

"Yes, ma'am," Paulina confirmed. She glanced to her left and caught Rosemary's pinched expression.

Mr. Thompson set his utensils down and leaned back on his chair, folding his hands together, "A last name like Jones, though, now that's a bit interesting. If you don't mind me asking—and, truly, I only ask out of curiosity—what is your father's... nationality?"

Paulina more than suspected that a different word almost took the place at the end of that sentence. Rosemary started to make a noise of protest, but Paulina answered regardless. "He's American. Born on this side," she said, trying to keep suspicion from creeping into her tone. Mr. Thompson still wasn't satisfied, though.

"So, he's white then?" he prodded.

"Pops!" Rosemary admonished her grandfather. "What does this have to do with anything?"

"Calm down, Rosie, I didn't mean anything by it. Paulina grew up here. I'm just curious about what that must have been like for her." He turned his attention back to Paulina, still expecting an answer.

She didn't have one to give him, though. Race wasn't usually anything she gave much thought to. She was from the Valley, and nearly everyone in the Valley was Mexican. The only gringos she knew were the children of diplomats that she went to school with, who moved to a different country every couple of years. And, of course, the snowbirds in front of her. Seasonal guests, usually gone before they could poke too many holes in the foundation of the status quo.

She answered the question as best she could "No, I wouldn't say so. He speaks Spanish, at least." Language was typically the real marker for who considered themselves Latino and who counted as 'Americanized.' In the Valley, though, where Spanish flowed freely, there were fourth-generation kids who still spoke like they came straight from el barrio.

Mr. Thompson nodded, saying nothing.

"The weather here is truly a marvel," Mrs. Thompson said, "fresh produce year-round, virtually no risk of frost, and no snow at all! I mean, just look at what a beautiful day we're having! Right in the middle of December. I'm sure hurricane season is a toss-up, but there hasn't been a big storm in decades, right?"

"That's right," Paulina agreed, "not since Dolly." She didn't add that that particular storm had all but torn the roof off of her parent's house. South Padre is a barrier island. When the sea took its revenge, it exacted a heavy toll.

"You are such a lucky girl to have grown up in a place as temperate as this. You've never even *seen* a winter." Mrs. Thompson reached over and added a second serving of salad to Paulina's plate, unprompted.

"And I've never seen a spring." Paulina smiled. But, when Mrs. Thompson only blinked and tilted her head in response, she realized that it was an odd thing to say. "I do count myself lucky, though, to have grown up right by the ocean," she amended.

Thankfully, Rosemary saw it fit to take over the situation and distracted her grandmother with talk of her upcoming classes. The rest of the meal passed without incident, sparing the moment when Mrs. Thompson suggested that perhaps Paulina could cook for them next time, as she'd love to try some new "ethnic" foods. Paulina winced in response, and Rosemary openly face-palmed, but the comment was forgotten by the time the table was cleared and the two girls were able to abscond to the nearby stretch of beach.

They walked along the ocean, just out of reach from the waves. Paulina shivered and rubbed the goosebumps from her arms. She hadn't noticed it during lunch, but the temperature must have dropped a few degrees since the morning.

"I am so sorry about… all of that," Rosemary said, kicking a clump of wet sand in front of her.

"Hey, no need to apologize. It was… definitely an experience, but not too bad— all things considered." Paulina found herself scanning the ground in front of her. She darted forward for a moment and returned with a piece of blue sea glass, its edges made soft by the steady wear of the waves. She gave it to Rosemary, who chewed on her bottom lip.

"You don't hate me for that, then? Really?"

Paulina laughed. "Please, you should hear the things we say about *y'all*."

Escúchame

Brownsville, Texas

1982

"Listen to me. I know English isn't your first language, but this cannot happen again. Do you hear me? If I hear you speak Spanish again, I will have you removed from the classroom."

Maria didn't look up from her shoes. She had been studying them for so long she was sure she would have the image of their white laces imprinted in her mind forever. Sister Gloria had been reprimanding her for the past ten minutes, and Maria's concentration was split between understanding the elderly nun and trying not to cry.

"Look at me. I need to know that you understand what I'm saying," she said. Sister Gloria did not flinch when Maria met her gaze with red-rimmed eyes.

"I understand," Maria said slowly, carefully sounding out each syllable.

"Don't make me embarrass you like this again." Sister Gloria jutted her chin towards the office door. "Now, go."

Maria snatched her backpack from the floor and left the office in a hurry. She did not stop to talk to anyone in the hallway. She kept her gaze forward and her back straight as she walked toward her locker, determined not to show her embarrassment. Still, she felt shame creep in with each step. It started as an uncomfortably warm feeling in her chest and spread throughout her whole body—from the tips of her fingers to her hairline. Though she was desperate to put distance between herself and Sister Gloria's office, Maria slowed her pace when she realized how quickly she was walking. She didn't want anyone to think that something was wrong.

Maria had started at Villa Maria entirely too late. Not only did she register in the middle of the school year, but she did so as an eighth grader, at fourteen years old. Unlike Maria, most of the other students at her school had been there since kindergarten and grew up speaking English.

Before transferring, Maria had prided herself on her perfect attendance and being the kind of student that teachers enjoyed having in class. But none of that mattered at her new school. She didn't know

English. There was no getting around it. The teacher's words crashed

over her and she struggled to pick and parse the few phrases that

sounded familiar to her.

Maria had tried not to let herself get overwhelmed by the

things she didn't know. She focused on the things within her control.

She asked her teachers for extra homework and read every elementary-

level book in the library to build her foundation. It didn't take long for

her to get a sense of the grammar. There was always a subject and a

verb, usually a direct or indirect object. Adjectives were a bit tricky

because they weren't gendered and usually came before the noun, not

after, but they were still manageable. The rules were easy enough to

remember, it was the words that evaded her. Her vocabulary in

English was so limited that she often found herself having to use five

words to make up for the one that she lacked. So instead of saying

"Did you understand yesterday's lesson?" she would have to say "Did

you understand the thing that the teacher talked about in class the day

before today?" Maria felt that she sounded like a child and she was

sure that everyone else thought the same.

Which was why, when she had to ask one of her classmates a question that morning, she answered it in her mother tongue. Because she had wanted, just for one second, to feel wholly and completely understood.

That classmate, Carolina, was standing in front of Maria's locker.

"Hey," Carolina said, as Maria fumbled with the lock, "I'm sorry about what happened. Sister Gloria shouldn't be so hard on you. She didn't even give you a warning!"

Carolina seemed indignant on her behalf, which was kind of her. The two girls weren't close, but they had grown up just down the street from each other. Carolina had been attending Villa Maria for almost ten years and Maria struggled with her jealousy over the girl's perfect, unaccented English. It was a bitter thing—her anger. She tried to keep out of her voice when she responded.

"It's fine, I shouldn't have spoken in Spanish. I'm here to learn, and I need to put better attention in class anyway." Maria realized her mistake a few seconds too late but tried to correct herself. "I meant pay. I need to pay better attention in class. Obviously." She finished in a deadpan, trying to play her mistake off as a joke. Thankfully, Carolina just smiled.

"Still, it wasn't right of her to do that." Carolina stepped forward so that she could whisper to Maria. "Lo siento."

Maria blinked hard as she watched Carolina walk away. She thought about how lo siento, though it meant "I'm sorry," could also be translated as "I feel it."

Maria wondered for the first time if she wasn't the only one grieving the loss of her language.

. . .

Maria made her way to the chapel that afternoon, after her confrontation with Sister Gloria. It would be a while before her mother could cross the border and pick her up, and she figured that she could use some guidance—any guidance.

The chapel was dark and empty. Maria entered it without turning on the lights. Late-afternoon sunlight poured through the stained-glass window behind the pulpit and colored the floor in front of her. She lit a candle at the altar and knelt at the first pew, unsure of how to begin. She thought, for a while, of the series of events that had led her to the chapel.

Attending Catholic school hadn't been Maria's idea. When her father was still alive, he insisted she attend school in Matamoros, her hometown, even when the other parents in their neighborhood started shuttling their kids across the border to go to school in the United States. He wanted her to get her education in Mexico, like the rest of her family. The revisionist in Maria believed that it was because her father thought she was fine the way she was, that she didn't need to learn English to be complete. In reality, it probably had more to do with him not wanting to wake up at five every morning to drive his daughter across the Río Bravo.

Maria's father had always been the short-term kind of practical. Unlike Maria's mother, who insisted that learning English could open doors for Maria down the line. Growing up, Maria had always heard her say, "Los que saben dos idiomas valen por dos." This was especially true on the border, where nearly everyone spoke with split tongues. Within a week of her father's death, Maria was transferred to Villa Maria.

It was difficult not to conflate the two events. In a manner of days, Maria had to navigate a world that lacked two fundamental constants—her father, her language. She missed them both. She missed them terribly. She missed them in a way that couldn't be divided and examined separately. She missed her father most when she thought of the way he would roll his r's when he called her "mi reina."

With his voice in her head, Maria made the sign of the cross and whispered to herself, "In the name of the Father, the Son, and the Saintly Spirit." She paused and corrected herself. "Holy Spirit."

With no one but God around to hear her, she spoke in stilted, broken English—the only kind that she had to offer.

"Dear God… I am sorry. I am trying very hard, but my English is not very good yet. Please, understand me anyway. I am not sure what I should do. I study, but don't know if it is functioning. I do not think I know enough to make it. I want to be better, but I do not know that *I* am enough. Diosito—God, would you let me know if I am enough?" Maria pled.

She thought of her father's funeral at the Santa Maria church back in Matamoros. The service had been in Spanish—had God heard her then? Or did He only listen closely when she suffered? Had she ever spoken to God in true fealty when the words came readily?

"God," Maria tried again, "I am not going to give up. You would not have put me here if I did not have the time to learn. There is time…" Maria didn't know how to phrase what she wanted to say next.

There was no English translation for "Yo me encargo," not really. How could she help God understand that she was determined to manage the situation, to resolve it no matter what it took away from her? How could she explain that she was ready to take responsibility for everything that came her way? The whole English language and there was no substitute for those three words.

Maria was about to get up, leaving her prayer unfinished, when she saw the lit candle begin to flicker. She thought of her father—of his endless work, his endless effort. This may not have been what he wanted for her, but he would have wanted her to try. She stared at the sunlight coming in through the stained-glass window until her eyes watered. Then, she closed them tightly and bowed her head one last time.

“It will get done,” Maria said finally.

WINTER TEXANS PART III

South Padre Island, Texas

2022

Four years passed. The friends reunited every December, without fail. They spent their winter breaks beach combing and stargazing. Paulina avoided the Thompson's house when she could, but held her tongue when she couldn't. If they wanted to ask invasive questions about her family or purse their lips when Paulina accidentally slipped and used Mexican slang around them, she figured it said more about their character than hers.

Besides, Rosemary never made her feel like she was less than for her background or the way she spoke. In fact, she had even told her how she picked up some of Paulina's phrases and started using them around her friends back home. Somewhere in a suburb of Detroit, there was a group of private school kids saying "no mames güey" whenever they wanted to express their profound disbelief. Paulina found the mental image too hilarious to try and stop it.

By the winter break of their senior year of high school, Rosemary finally convinced her grandparents to let her spend New Year's Eve with her friend. Paulina planned to take her to a bonfire party out on Boca Chica Beach. It was an annual thing, but usually reserved for upperclassmen. It wasn't until her last year of high school that Paulina finally knew someone who knew someone who knew and shared the location of the party.

Paulina rolled to a stop at the end of the Thompson's long, winding driveway. It was already past sunset, so she signaled her arrival with two quick honks of her horn. After a few moments, Rosemary appeared on the front porch, kicking the door shut behind her. She raced down the steps, skipping the last one.

"Oh my god, you actually got the car!" Rosemary said as she slid into the passenger seat.

"Bought her this morning." Paulina grinned. "This'll be her maiden voyage. With me, anyway."

After two years of working at a local souvenir shop, Paulina finally raised enough money to buy herself a new, used car. The 2005 Honda Civic wasn't a fancy ride by anyone's standards, but it ran, it got great gas mileage, and, most importantly, it was *hers*.

"You must be so proud of yourself." Rosemary reached over and squeezed Paulina's knee. "*I* am so proud of you."

Paulina's heart sang, and she kept smiling as they drove across the bridge that connected South Padre Island to the mainland. Boca Chica Beach was on the other side of the bay, east of Brownsville and down close to the border. It had taken a fair bit of cajoling to get Rosemary's grandparents to let her go so far out on her own. Paulina's parents hadn't inquired about her New Year's Eve plans, but she left them a note on the counter all the same.

The girls listened to all of their favorite songs on the long drive. Their shared music blog had fallen off after a couple of years but neither of them quite outgrew their garage band punk music days. It was dark by the time they found the right place, and Paulina was so content she had forgotten that the night was just beginning.

The bonfire burned brightly, throwing sparks into the winter night. The light it emitted did nothing to dim the stars, though. Where they were, nestled away in the last corner of the coast, the light pollution peeled away to reveal whole, glistening constellations. Rosemary pointed out Orion, her favorite, as soon as they got out of the car. The whole sky was a tapestry of diamond-stars, a stark contrast to the crowd of stumbling, intoxicated teenagers.

Paulina pulled her oversized hoodie down over her legs and half-retreated into the sleeves. She had paired it with her favorite shorts—an outfit that should have been warm enough, given the bonfire—but the night was colder than she had expected. She stood close to Rosemary, trying to draw from her heat.

The two girls hovered around the fire, hesitant to join any one group. Paulina waved at a few people she recognized from her high school and it wasn't long before someone handed her a half-empty liquor bottle. She couldn't read the label in the low light.

"What is that?" Rosemary asked.

"Not sure, but it looks clear. Maybe vodka?" Paulina wiped the rim of the bottle with the sleeve of her hoodie and took a swig. It was a battle to keep it down. It tasted like a boiled leather shoe. "A la verga. No way that's vodka." Paulina gagged.

A drunk girl materialized next to Paulina. Sofia Mendoza, from her government class. "Mensa, you just chugged mezcal." She hiccupped, swaying on her feet.

"Güey, que te cuesta decirme *antes*." She tried to hand her the bottle, but Rosemary intercepted it.

"May as well." She shrugged and took a conservative sip. Her whole face scrunched up, but she kept it down without so much as a cough. "That was… bracing."

"That's one way to put it," Paulina grumbled. The taste was awful, but already she could feel a warmth spreading from the middle of her chest down to her fingertips. She took another sip from the bottle, and Sofia stumbled off before she could hand it over.

Neither Rosemary nor Paulina had drunk before, outside of communion wine, and it didn't take long for it to go to their heads. They broke away from the party, heading toward the sand dunes, before ever really making an effort to join it. But what were parties with strangers if not the social ritual required to obtain free booze?

The girls climbed up a tall sand dune. Halfway to the peak, Rosemary fell to her knees and kept going on a three-legged crawl, holding the mezcal bottle up over her head. Paulina took it from her, holding its neck by the very tips of her fingers. She spun around on her heel and plopped down on the sand. Rosemary joined her, leaning her head on Paulina's shoulder. Her hair smelled like eucalyptus and mint. It tickled Paulina's nose.

"I miss you when I leave, you know?"

"I know."

"Do you miss me?"

"So much."

"Good." Rosemary nestled closer to Paulina, almost like she wanted to climb into her hoodie with her. "It doesn't have to be like this forever, you know. We could go to the same college. The same state, at least."

Paulina absorbed the suggestion in silence. If she wanted to, she could point out that she and Rosemary didn't exactly have the same options when it came to their education. Rosemary was practically born with a college fund; she could go anywhere she wanted. Paulina had to contend with moving costs and loans and choosing a major that would pull her out of her inevitable debt. She wouldn't be able to leave Texas—hell, she probably wouldn't even be able to leave the Valley. The last thing she wanted to do was trap Rosemary with her. She could have pointed it out, but she didn't. The things unsaid between them went unsaid for a reason.

Besides, she liked things the way they were, their familiar patterns. Having Rosemary at arm's length, up north for most of the year, was miles better than the solitude that she had known in the years before meeting her. Better than coming home to an empty house for the fourth night in a row and having to conclude that it was because of her. That her parents just didn't want to be around *her*. Being with Rosemary full-time, though, Paulina just wasn't sure if she was ready for that. She was so sure that if it happened, if she wanted it badly enough to make it happen, Rosemary would just get sick of her and leave again. This time, of her own volition.

"It was just a thought…" Rosemary murmured, her eyes closed.

Paulina felt a very physical pain in her heart. "It's a good thought. Hold on to that one." She took one last gulp from the bottle, draining the dregs. Finally, she was drunk enough not to taste it.

Paulina laid back in the sand, and Rosemary did the same. If she closed her eyes and listened to the waves lapping on the shore, she could almost imagine that she was out there— floating in the dark abyss. Even as she lay perfectly still, her whole body swayed. After a while, when she finally spoke, her words spilled out of her in a torrent.

"You know, when I was a kid, they always told me that birds fly south for the winter. Well, there's no real 'they,' I guess, but my third-grade science teacher definitely said it once or twice. What was her name? Mrs. Bonnet? Bennet? Anyway, doesn't matter. That year, I did a poster board on black-bellied whistling ducks. How they fly south for the winter. Cool stuff. But then winter came a few months later and I kept looking up at the sky, waiting to see the black-bellied whistling ducks flying overhead. But there was nothing there. Nada. Los cielos vacíos." Paulina turned to look at Rosemary. Her eyes were closed and her breaths were slow and steady. She could have been asleep. Paulina continued, anyway. "But get this, then I look down. I look at the resacas—what we call lakes here—and *asu madre,* so many birds! Filling every pond and spilling over onto the sidewalks and streets. So many black-bellied whistling ducks. Anyway," she slurred, "it was 'round then that I figured it out."

"Figured what out?" Rosemary whispered, her eyes still closed.

"That this is as south as south goes. That I was born in the place where things end up," she said, her voice low, "people come, but no one stays."

Rosemary reached over and took Paulina's hand in hers. Finally, she opened her eyes, and Paulina saw all the stars reflected back at her "I'll stay," Rosemary said, "I'll stay with you, this time, I promise."

The two girls stayed out there in the dunes long after the party was over and the bonfire had burned to embers. They stayed until they sobered up, and they watched the sunrise over the Gulf of Mexico. They drove back to the island in comfortable silence, their favorite songs playing softly over the speakers. When Paulina finally pulled up to the Thompsons' driveway, both of Rosemary's grandparents were waiting on the porch. Nana looked relieved to see them alive and well, but Mr. Thompson glared at her with a fury that could have leveled entire fields.

Paulina parked the car, and Rosemary reached across the console to squeeze her hand. "Don't worry about them, I'll handle it."

"They're going to be pissed."

"They'll get over it."

"They're going to be pissed at *me*."

"Paulina," Rosemary said intently, "it's going to be okay."

Rosemary got out of the car before Paulina could get another word in. She closed the door gently behind herself and gave her friend one last reassuring smile before climbing up the porch steps and motioning her grandparents inside.

Paulina spent the rest of that winter break alone. Mr. Thompson was furious that they stayed out all night, and blamed Paulina. Rosemary offered platitudes, but no solutions. By early January, the Thompsons returned to their home in Michigan. Paulina returned to her part-time job and her last semester of high school classes.

The following year, it snowed.

AND BEYOND

Brownsville, Texas

2023

Sandra had fallen asleep much later than intended. Her husband, Manuel, was away on a business trip to Mexico City, and she had stayed on the phone with him until well past midnight. They talked about how his presentation went—he was the keynote speaker for the Sociedad Psicoanalítica de México—and she made him promise he would stop by her Tia Lucinda's apartment para merendar before he left the city.

She updated her husband on her week. Sandra had recently RSVPed "yes" for their goddaughter's wedding in Matamoros, despite Homeland Security holding up the paperwork to renew their Sentri— the program that allowed them expedited travel over the International Bridge, as frequent crossers. They had missed too many big events in the political mess of the last few years, Sandra argued, and it was time they suck it up and deal with the lines. If Border Patrol wanted to painstakingly inspect every inch of their minivan, that would just be the cost of catching up with their friends from the other side.

"Ahí vemos," said Manuel, "but if we get stuck in a 3-hour line at the bridge, we're taking turns behind the wheel."

Sandra agreed, then complained, at length, about the traffic on 802. With so many Californians moving in from out of state, it was starting to take half a lifetime to get from one side of town to the other. All of Brownsville's major streets were clogged with Teslas and their drivers, who were too scared of being ticketed to speed the expected amount.

"No es por nada," Sandra said over speaker phone, as she used both hands to pet the family dog, "pero we're a small town for a reason! We don't have the infrastructure for all these gringos. Te lo juro they're going to run us out of town… and they're probably gonna eat all of our avocados first, too, aren't they? Yes, they are. I know they are." She directed her complaints at Baldo, who looked at her with eyes of canine adoration and very little understanding.

Her husband laughed, but reminded her that the Californians were probably a good thing. White people moving in was a sign of a healthy economy—at least, that's what the mayor kept telling them. It had started as a small trickle, just a family or two, but in the last couple of years the change had become noticeable. Something you could point to. Stores and restaurants opened up to cater to the new clientele, and Sandra found herself handing over 20-dollar bills so that her kids could go buy boba tea at the newest strip mall.

When Sandra finished airing her grievances, they circled back to the wedding and discussed if it would be worth having the kids drive down for it. The two of them spoke until Manuel's voice grew raspy and Sandra forgot about the half-empty mug of té de manzanilla on her nightstand. She slept as she often did when she was home alone, in the middle of the bed, with Baldo curled up at her feet.

Sandra dreamt that she was standing beneath an anacahuita tree, waiting for her husband to come home. Then the tree rained white petals all around her, and she smiled, until she looked down and saw that the petals had turned into a pile of dead birds lying at her feet.

Sandra woke up to the inexplicable sound of crashing.

She jolted up in bed. The bedroom windows rattled in their frames, and the books and knick-knacks that decorated her bookcase shook so fervently the colors blurred. Above her, a framed seascape painting swayed back and forth, threatening to fall off its hook. She scrambled off the bed before it could crack her head open. Her legs tangled in the bedsheets and she fell onto the floor.

Baldo stood by the open bedroom door, whining quietly. Sandra scooped him up and ran into the kitchen, where her nice wedding china had spilled onto the floor—shattered into long pieces of white porcelain. The ground continued to shake beneath her, and she didn't know what to do. Should she hide in the basement? Or is that what people did for tornadoes?

There were no earthquakes in Brownsville. Hurricanes, yes. Flash floods, occasionally. But never, ever an earthquake.

Sandra thought of the terremoto that struck Mexico City back in the '85. It killed thousands. Her Tia Lucinda's house had crumbled into nothing.

In the end, she wrenched open the back door and ran into the yard—she didn't want to be inside if the house collapsed. The tremors subsided, but Sandra was greeted by a sight stranger than an earthquake in South Texas: an ash-gray plume that cut through the hazy autumn morning.

"Mierda," she whispered to herself, bending down to drop the dog gently onto the grass.

She considered the possibilities: Had war come to Brownsville? There was war in Europe, war in the Middle East, but who had anything to gain from bombing a border town?

Back inside the house, Sandra's phone flooded with messages.

. . .

Father Luis was familiar with the sight of vacant pews. Though almost no one showed up for the 7:00 a.m. Mass, he insisted on opening the heavy oak doors of the church to the public. He was an old man—set in his ways and privileged with seniority. He knew, from experience, that there would always be someone there to listen— maquiladora and construction workers who wanted to take the Eucharist and break their fasts before long shifts, young parents who knew their children wouldn't fall back asleep anyway, Marist Brothers who taught at the local Catholic school. For as long as there were people willing to hear the word of God, he would be there to speak it.

The priest rolled his shoulders and straightened his back before starting down the aisle for the opening procession. He kept his gaze forward, but from the corner of his eye he took stock of everyone in the room: three factory workers to his left, and a young woman with a baby cradled in her arms to his right. He knew most of them by sight, if not by name. Alone in the front pew sat someone that the priest did not recognize— a redheaded young man. His hands, covered in freckles, were knotted tightly on his lap. Father Luis nodded to him as he passed by.

He reached the sanctum at the front of the room and heard the first few notes of "Morning has Broken" played over the piano. His niece, Julia, was the band director at St. Ignatius and could always be counted on to attend the early morning masses. Though they lacked a full choir, the music was enough to set the tone for the service. He bowed to the altar and moved behind it, pressing his lips to the cloth that covered the marble. It was cool to the touch.

As the last notes played out, filling the hall of the lord, Father Luis cleared his throat and began the introductory rites.

"Bienvenidos. Welcome, everyone." The priest smiled. "In the name of the Father, the Son, and of the Holy Spirit." He made the sign of the cross, and those assembled in front of him followed his lead.

"Amen," they chorused back.

"The grace of our Lord, Jesus Christ, and the love of God, and the communion of the Holy Spirit be with you all," he said.

"And with your spirit," they responded.

"Together, we pray: I confess to Almighty God and to you, my brothers and sisters, that I have sinned." He pressed a closed fist to his chest. "In my thoughts and in my words, in what I have done and what I have failed to do. And I ask the Blessed Mary, ever virgin, and all the angels and saints and you, my brothers and sisters, to pray for me to the Lord our God." Luis had begun the Penitential Act alone, but as he progressed, the rest of the congregation joined their voices to his.

The beginning of Mass passed without incident. He preached on the importance of being a good neighbor and outlined the parable of the Good Samaritan. He made the point that our neighbor is everyone around us, regardless of their background, and emphasized that, as comforting as it was to exist in a close-knit community, they should not remain cloistered. God's embrace, and Sacred Heart Catholic Church, welcomed all. This earned him a smile from the newcomer in the front row.

He went through the routine faithfully, as he did all things. It was only when he got to the liturgy of the Eucharist that Father Luis felt the first press of exhaustion.

He had led hundreds of Masses over the years. The people changed, but their faults and their worries never did. Largely, the lessons he taught stayed the same. He knew it was not his place to question the will of God, but as Father Luis prepared the body and blood of Christ, he wondered when—*if*—things would change. He wondered when they all would learn.

His hands shook as he lifted the chalice up to heaven. "Blessed… blessed are you, Lord, God of all creation…" He tightened his grip as wine threatened to spill over the rim of the cup, but when he heard cries of confusion from the congregation, he realized that it was the entire room that shook, not just his weathered hands.

Father Luis placed the chalice on the altar, where it fell over and rolled onto the floor. Red wine sank into the carpet like a bloodstain, but the priest was already running down the steps to the aisle between pews, where the few church members had flocked. Above them, a light fixture swayed and flickered. The young woman's baby cried; its wails pierced through the intermittent darkness.

"Asu chingada madre," one of the maquiladora workers swore, "is it an earthquake?"

"Can't be. There aren't any terremotos in Brownsville," responded one of his compadres, who held onto the back of a pew with both hands—knuckles white as he struggled to remain upright.

"Güey, what else do you call it when the ground shakes?"

Father Luis felt a tug on his sleeve. "Tío, what is this?" asked Julia.

The priest's thoughts flickered back to the moment before the shaking began—the heaviness he felt, and his desire for change. His words laced with fear and reverence, Father Luis whispered, "The Rapture."

The young woman, who had been silent until now, let out a choked sob. "It's too soon!" She cried. "Padre, por favor. His baptism isn't until December. Please, help us."

Though Father Luis had not been able to put a name to the woman before, he recognized her now as Beatrice Mendoza. She had completed all of her sacraments in this church—including, most recently, the sacrament of marriage. Her son, Tómas, was to be baptized in less than a month.

"Damé el niño." Father Luis took the squalling baby in his arms and motioned for everyone gathered to follow him to the front of the room. When he saw the lone young man still sitting in the front row, hunched over and with his freckled hands covering the back of his head, he called over his shoulder, "Mijo, come with us." The young man heard him and, tentatively, followed.

Father Luis led his procession back down the aisle, though the Mass was still unfinished. All around them, Bibles fell out of their cubbies and thudded onto the floor like dulled gunfire. The religious iconography that had decorated the sacred walls of the church for nearly a century came crashing down. The overhead lights had gone out entirely, but Father Luis followed the light of the stained-glass window, which pooled in whorls of blue and red before the church entrance. The world swayed beneath his creaking knees, but the priest did not falter.

He led the group to a basin of holy water at the front of the room, where church members were encouraged to dip their fingers and bless themselves before entering the hall of the Lord. He asked those gathered to hold hands and surround him and the child. In an emergency, the only things required for baptism were water and the words.

He addressed the group: "We are gathered here under the protection of God. Be not afraid. We bless this child so that he may walk in the light of the Lord, come what may."

With one arm, and more strength than he thought was left to him, he held the baby over the basin. He dipped a cupped hand into the water and poured it over the baby's brow three times as he said the words, "Tómas, I baptize you in the name of the Father, and of the Son, and of the Holy Spirit."

The baby stopped crying and looked up at the priest with curious eyes as the shaking finally subsided.

Father Luis turned back to the altar, where he had been when the presumed rapture began. The crucifix that hung behind it remained fixed in place. Above it, a crack in the plaster—dark, as hungry as a mouth.

…

Oscar's mother had insisted he go further north.

"Mijo, tu sigelé," she had told him, when he left Venezuela, "when you cross the border, you keep going until it's *safe*."

But Oscar's passage through Central America and México had been long, and not without danger. When the opportunity to rest finally came, he took it with both hands.

Even though Oscar had gone to school for political science, he started working on a construction site soon after arriving in Brownsville. It was a job that paid, and the man who hired him didn't ask too many questions. Since the construction site was nearly 40 minutes outside of town, Oscar usually hitched a ride with the other crew members.

The guys warmed up to him after a couple afternoons of working together under the sweltering Texas sun. The dynamics of the group were familiar, reminding him of his friends back home. They joked around, helped each other out, had each other's backs—especially if someone caught wind that immigration officials would be showing up at the site. After a week on the job, he knew all their soccer teams and what their wives packed them for lunch. In that, there was almost a brotherhood.

Early on a November morning, an hour before the sun broke over the horizon, Oscar waited outside his apartment complex, where he rented an unfurnished studio the size of a large closet. He had gotten his first American paycheck a couple days before (more accurately, his first American wad-of-cash-stuffed-into-a-torn-envelope). After sending most of the money to his mother and paying his rent for the next month, he found that he still had a little left over.

The smell of coffee wafted up to him as he waited. He had woken up extra early that morning to order five black coffees from the Whataburger a couple blocks over—one for each of the guys that he rode with. When Angel rolled up in his rusted, red pickup truck, Oscar handed the drink carrier over to Pancho before clambering up to join him and Juan in the truck bed.

"Orale! What's the occasion?" Pancho asked.

Oscar squinted at him. He often struggled to pick up English phrases, but luckily the other guys on the crew mixed enough Spanish into their speech that he usually got by.

"Nomas sé me antojo," Oscar shrugged. Once he settled into his cramped spot between the wheel well and the back of the truck bed, he passed two drinks through the open window to Angel and David, who rode up front. The guys thanked him, and the group of them set off east.

Oscar had caught Pancho and Juan in the middle of a conversation. Juan, who was from Colombia and whose accent most closely resembled Oscar's, was explaining how, though he had saved enough money to bring his wife and kids over to the States, she wasn't sure if she wanted to come.

"Si la entiendo, don't get me wrong. I know the journey is hard and she'll have the boys with her, pero como no entiende that there's nothing *left* for us in Colombia?" Juan ran a hand through his short hair. "¡Ya, basta! It's time to go."

"No sé, güey, tal vez no es tiempo," Angel reasoned, "might be better to just wait 'til things settle down a little bit."

Oscar took a long sip of his coffee and closed his eyes, resting his head against the back of the truck. He let their conversation wash over him, having understood enough to know what they were really talking about—the worth of home, and the cost of leaving it.

It had taken Oscar a decade to find the courage to flee Caracas. Most of his cousins left in 2013, when things were bad, but not desperate. Five years later, though, the desperate turned to violence, and the capital of his beloved nation had become uninhabitable. Crime ran rampant throughout the city. Motorcycle gangs patrolled the streets and jumped anyone who looked like an easy target. The situation was simple enough on paper: The country was out of food, and hunger was a demon. It ground people down to their barest instincts and made them resort to things they would never do with the comfort of a full belly.

The day Oscar arrived in the US, he was hungry. With just enough money left to buy a couple more meals and a bus ticket going north, he didn't intend to linger in Texas. He had the paperwork to get through the immigration checkpoint in Sarita, and after that, it would be a matter of reaching a sanctuary city and finding work.

Having crossed the border, though, Oscar was struck by how similar it all was. The same palm trees dotted the landscape on either side of the Rio Grande. The people looked the same. They sounded the same. When he ducked into a restaurant at a strip mall, *Gorditas Doña Tota,* he was greeted in Spanish without question: "Buenas tardes, ¿qué le gustaría?"

Oscar's first bite of a gordita brought tears to his eyes. It tasted so close to the arepas that his mother used to make, before the food shortages. It reminded him of what he had left behind, and made him realize how much of it was still here waiting for him—in a border town that felt like an almost-home.

As harsh as his reality in Venezuela had been, his days dictated by gangs and rolling blackouts, Oscar had struggled to leave. He loved his country and the family that remained to him. And, unlike most of his friends, he had spent much of his twenties holding on to hope— hope that the government was only one fair election away from turning things around, hope that his community would pull through, hope that fear wouldn't turn them all against their neighbors. But by the time Oscar found the will to leave his aging mother, things were so bad that the government had stopped reporting the homicide rates.

Oscar stayed quiet for most of the car ride. But before they unloaded the truck, he caught Juan by the elbow.

"Le va a calar a tu esposa, pero sí traelos," Oscar advised, "ya que ella llegué, te va entender." When he spoke, Oscar thought of his first night sleeping in the US, and how quiet it had been.

The five of them walked over to the foreman to clock in and get their orders for the first half of their shift. The work they did was hard, but Oscar enjoyed it. Back home, where jobs were scarce, his hands had itched for something to do. Here, there was always a next step. Break some ground. Lay some pipes. Pave a road. The crew did a little bit of everything, and the management team had people working around the clock. To Oscar, it seemed like they were building a whole city from scratch.

While he was on the site, it was easy for Oscar to understand the work in front of him. The foreman and his compadres always explained how to do each task clearly and in Spanish. Soon, though, he noticed how all the actual planning happened behind closed doors, in English. Routinely, white men in suits came down to the site to track their progress. They walked among the construction workers—picking their way through rubble in their slippery dress shoes—but spoke only to each other.

Oscar spent the first hour of his shift roofing the newest addition to their small city—an office building that towered over the surrounding land. Since the work didn't require any loud equipment, the crew chatted as they worked. It made the day go faster. Pancho's daughter was having her quinceñera the following summer, and he wanted everyone's opinion on whether it would be worth saving up for a venue or if they should just keep it small and do it in the backyard.

As they talked, Oscar stopped to admire the view. From twelve stories up, he could easily look out over the Gulf Coast. This ocean was a darker blue than he was used to, but the brackish scent of it drove a stab of nostalgia through his heart as he thought of his childhood spent next to the Caribbean Sea.

If he looked to the south, past the miles of untamed grass and shrubbery, he could make out a glint of green—the curve of the Rio

Grande. Between them and the river stood a thousand acres of protected land: Las Palomas Wildlife Management Area. The only reason he knew about it was because of Pancho's daughter, the soon-to-be-quinceñera.

A month earlier, Pancho had come to work waving around a piece of paper—a petition that his daughter wanted them all to sign, one that would stop the development of land close to the wildlife preserve. She was worried about the bird population, he claimed, and had worked herself to tears thinking about how they were going to destroy the existing nesting habitat.

The crew had laughed it off, Pancho included. They weren't about to risk the jobs that put food on their tables. Oscar didn't sign the petition either, but he wished he could have. He wished he didn't live in a world where the only way to survive was to destroy.

Oscar was deep in thought when the bombs went off.

The noise was deafening, and it shocked him senseless. He dropped to the ground, curling into a fetal position to protect his organs. A sharp pain pierced his left side. He squeezed his eyes shut so tightly that he saw white. He heard the commotion. His friends shouted over the noise. The tools and supplies they had been using just minutes before clattered all around him as the newly finished building shook and swayed.

In the chaos, Oscar was pulled back to a moment a decade prior, when he and two of his school friends—Carlos and Miguelito—protested the Maduro administration. The three of them had hatched a plan to hole up in a government building for a couple of days. They weren't planning to vandalize it or anything. They just wanted to make it harder for officials to do their jobs—jobs that they were already doing so poorly in the first place.

But some official got impatient, or else the wrong officer got wind of their encampment. Early in the morning on their second day of protest, someone busted open the front door to the building's lobby and threw in a bomb. The boys, still half asleep, didn't have time to react. Carlos lost his sight, and Miguelito his life. For months afterwards, Oscar could hear the sound that the bomb made when it detonated every time he closed his eyes.

Hearing that noise now, in the United States, where he was supposed to be safe, Oscar could only think that his mother had been right. Crossing the river meant nothing, when violence followed.

Oscar stayed on the ground until the shaking subsided, but it did subside, and his only injuries had come from falling onto an overturned box of nails. Through the haze, he could make out Juan's outstretched hand.

"Ánadale, amigo, you're okay." He hauled Oscar up and brushed the dirt off of him. "You're gonna be okay."

The air was thick with dust and smoke, and Oscar could no longer see the horizon.

. . .

On November 18th, 2023, at 7:32 a.m. Central Standard Time, SpaceX, an American space technology company, initiated the launch of Starship Ship 25 from their headquarters on Boca Chica Beach, Texas. The spacecraft was intended to attain near-orbital trajectory and return to earth in a controlled reentry over the Pacific Ocean, while a booster rocket completed a boostback burn and landed in the Gulf of Mexico. In total, the mission was meant to take 90 minutes.

The spacecraft achieved liftoff and successfully underwent stage separation.

However, the booster rocket experienced multiple engine failures and exploded during its boostback burn. In total, the launch lasted fewer than 9 minutes.

The company issued a statement calling the explosion a "rapid unscheduled disassembly," and claimed the mission as a victory on the journey to commercial space travel.

FOR THE LOVE OF GOD

Brownsville, Texas

2014

In the name of the Father, the Son,
and the Holy Spirit…

There's little dignity in exhaustion.

I was late for class this morning. Again. Normally I wouldn't have felt so bad about it, pero me da cosa con Brother David. He's teaching Bible Studies again this year and I hate to see him disappointed in me. But really, who is willingly reading the Old Testament first thing on a Thursday morning?

I sat next to Sol in class. She'd usually give me a hard time for being late, but she let it slide today. I think she saw how tired I was. Little Valeria still isn't sleeping through the night and I've been helping out Liliana while she's working at the hospital——trying to be a good

Tía and everything. Things aren't great right now, as I'm sure You can imagine.

Mom is… in shock, I guess. She's unresponsive. She's been like that since Dad took the last of his things on Sunday. He came while we were at church, the coward, and took everything he could fit into his mistress's tiny apartment.

Dad's house key was sitting on the kitchen table when we arrived from mass. Mom's face turned white when she saw it and she went straight into their room—her room. She hasn't spoken a word since then. Dad's called a couple of times. Never to apologize, but he has no shortage of excuses. He was unhappy, he felt stuck, he needed a change… I swear, every call just plants another seed of anger in my heart. It's bad enough he abandoned his family, he shouldn't feel the need to make us feel like we deserved it. This morning, I decided to just stop picking up.

I know, I know that I'm supposed to honor my parents, both of them, but I think You can take my side on this one.

Anyway, Lili and Valeria moved in the same day that Dad moved out, so let's just say that the dust hasn't really settled yet. We're doing our best. Liliana helps with Mom. I help with the baby. We're keeping our heads above water. Ahí vemos.

I'm praying because I'm tired, and I need a little bit of strength. Just enough to get through the end of the school day. I feel awful praying just because I need something, but I'm trying to be pragmatic here. You are the omnipotent creator of heaven and earth. I don't think You would have gone through all that trouble if You didn't have a little more to give.

We all just need an extra breath right now, don't we?

Please, Diosito.

En el nombre del padre, del hijo,
y del espíritu santo…

Okay, things might be on the upswing. My day got better, at least. Maybe it was the chocolate protein bar that Sol slipped into the pocket of my hoodie, maybe it was just being away from home for a couple of hours. Either way, I started to feel more normal as the day went on. Thank You, for that.

Classes went by quickly enough. Got my grade back in Physics and it could've been a lot worse, all things considered. After Mr. Miller's class, my last period, a bunch of us girls hung around the courtyard before heading home. It was the first day of autumn and the weather was gorgeous. It wasn't quite brisk enough to warrant a uniform-compliant cardigan, but even 80 degrees was a nice break from the relentless heatwave that spanned most of the summer.

Diana and Daniella, the twins, brought up the topic of homecoming, and Sol and I exchanged eye rolls that went unnoticed. It's not the idea of a school formal that I oppose. I think that getting dolled up and spending a night dancing actually sounds quite nice in theory. It's just the social ritual of it all that I can't get behind. Maybe it's the Catholic school factor, but the whole thing seems incredibly archaic. A boy chooses a girl that he wants to deign with his presence for a night, he lets his buddies know that she's off-limits, then he presents her with some minor token of affection that she's obligated to accept. I've seen what happens when a girl turns a guy down. It usually ends with her being called an ungrateful bi—

Perdóname, Diosito, no cursing.

Anyway, the topic was discussed ad infitum. Everyone hopes that the "right" guy will ask them to the dance, but no one ever entertains the idea that maybe *they* could pick the guy and ask *him*. Even better, they could avoid the Axe-deodorant-wearing chauvinists altogether, and go as a group—probably having a lot more fun in the process. It seems like the obvious solution to me, but I try not to be too judgmental about it. Just look at what happened with Mom and Dad. It's not girls' fault that we were socialized to be passive, to be prizes, while men get to call all the shots.

Sol walked me to my car afterward. She had stayed quiet for most of the homecoming conversation, but once we were alone she got *so* animated while talking about the upcoming community service project. She's been a member of the campus ministry group since August and she finally got Brother Michael to put her in charge of organizing the Marist Day of Service. She grinned so wide when she told me about it. She's thrilled to be assigning the service sites after three years of being stuck running the canned food drive.

It's kind of endearing, how invested she is. Me da ternura.

I mean, I've been participating in the Day of Service since I was twelve, it's the easiest way to collect service hours, pero I can't say I've ever cared much about where I ended up. Brother Micheal usually sets us up all over Brownsville, and the student body does everything from running clothing drives to spooning out food at the soup kitchen. I'm a good little Catholic, I'll follow instructions with the best of them, but it looks like Sol is determined to assign both of us to Garden Clean-Up in the Grotto.

I told her not to stress about it, that I would go wherever she put me, but she insisted that I would be most helpful in the garden. I tried to protest, but then she claimed that she just wanted the "joy of my company," with the usual sarcasm. She gave me a playful hip-bump as she said it, though. Sol is just like that, sometimes. A lot more…

physical than I'm used to. She's all about the hip-bumps and hand-holding and best-friend-cheek-kisses. I don't mind so much when it's coming from her, even if it did take me by surprise when we met back in elementary school.

We were nine, then. I had transferred into St. Ignatius three weeks into the Spring semester, after Mom had finally convinced Dad to cough up the tuition money. We were about to start a dancing unit in PE in preparation for the Charro Days festival. I was standing off in the corner of the gym, embarrassed because I didn't have a partner and didn't know who to ask. Sol abandoned hers—poor, freckled Ricky Martinez—and took my hand, no questions asked. She taught me how to dance como una Veracruzeña while I blushed scarlet. We were just kids, the stakes were low, and Sol showed me how to stop feeling so ashamed of myself all the time.

Sorry, I'm just rambling now. Anyway, I'm looking forward to the Day of Service. My full respect to the Marist brothers, but the garden at the Grotto is a *mess*. With everything going on at home, I know getting up to my elbows in soil will be a good distraction. It's like my Abuelita always said, nada cura como la tierra y el aire libre. And

Sol will be there. That helps too.

I have to confess, though, that I feel a bit guilty. I shouldn't be

so ready to help out here knowing what state Mom's garden is in right

now. It's normally maintained to perfection, but she hasn't been going

outside much these days. I watch Lili watch the weeds creep into the

low flower beds. She doesn't say anything, so I don't say anything, but

she must be waiting for me to pick up the slack.

I should. I want to. I should want to. But… gardening is one of

those sacred things, You know? Sacred enough that I don't want it to

feel like penance.

No, but I'll do it. Maybe it'll give Mom some strength. Maybe

it'll make up for everything. Somehow.

Either way, thank You for listening. And helping me through

the day.

En el nombre del padre, del hijo,
y del espíritu santo…

In the name of the Father, the Son,
and the Holy Spirit…

Hi, God.

So, I know it's been a couple days, but I'm driving home from school right now and I can't stop thinking about Mr. Miller's physics lesson from earlier, when he brought up the Multiverse Theory. The gist of it is that there is an infinite number of varied universes, right? So, there's a version of this universe where they served pizza in the cafeteria today instead of lasagna. And one where I showed up to school wearing a penguin costume. And a version where they serve pizza, I wear a penguin costume, *and* Mr. Miller doesn't even bother with the physics lesson because he teaches at a Catholic school and half of his students still believe in Creationism.

But I digress.

It did get me thinking, though—about how we're called to mitigate our faith with science. How are we supposed to believe that there are multiple versions of ourselves out there, all doing different things, when You are supposed to guide the path we walk? Could we really have been made in Your image and then remade a thousand times over?

I have my own theory. If life is a story, then maybe all of the alternate universes are just abandoned plotlines. Every alternate reality is another page scattered under Your desk. You could take us anywhere in this story, but You know exactly where we're going to end up. I like to think You chose this version of me.

But that's entirely wishful thinking. It's just another way of contextualizing, of finding purpose. Of finding a place for the pain, really. It's our suffering that cleanses us, right? It's what gets us into heaven, within reach of Your embrace.

Anyway, I'm rambling. And, also, pulling into the garage.

En el nombre del padre, del hijo,
y del espíritu santo…

It's two in the morning. It's two in the morning, and I can hear my mother sobbing from the other room. It's the first noise I've heard her make in almost two weeks. I can't sleep. So walk through this with me, please.

My mother did everything right. When she was married to my father, I swear she did everything right.

She never sent him to work without a packed lunch. She made her tortillas by hand. Her salsa verde never came out of a jar—I was with her when she planted the jalapeño seeds in the garden. She had two healthy children for him. She taught us Spanish and took us to church every Sunday. She did everything she was supposed to do.

And still, he left her.

He took her jewelry when he left. Everything he could find. Not that she ever hid anything from him. The only thing he doesn't have now is her wedding ring. Twenty-six years, and it never left her finger. She got to keep that, at least.

In the version of events where this killed her—where this actually killed her—I hope he didn't take the ring off her corpse. I hope he left it with the rest of us.

Pinche malcriado.

I'm sorry. God, I am so sorry.

Dios, please take this anger from me. I have no place for it.

En el nombre del padre, del hijo,

y del espíritu santo…

There's something distinctly soothing about pruning a citrus tree. Something in the scent of the orange blossoms and the easy monotony of it. I could write poems about the way the branches fall in a circle at my feet. How new beams of light dapple the grass with every cut I make. How it might hurt the tree, but it's what it needs. It needs to be cut back if it's going to grow tall—that's just the way of things.

I'm praying because it's also soothing, de una manera. Even if You don't respond in a way that makes sense right now, there's comfort in knowing that someone listens.

Sol is around here somewhere, wrangling freshmen into very respectfully power-washing the statue of the Virgin Mary that stands in the center of the grotto. It's surrounded by large paving stones that are currently overrun by weeds, but I haven't been able to convince any of the underclassmen to start pulling them. Most of them are focused on the more fun activities. For the girls, that means arranging the annual flowers that we bought into the pattern that we'll plant them in. For the boys, it's goading each other into trying to lift the cement benches that line the garden. They're there so that students can sit in silence while they pray to Mary, there's no reason to move them, but I've found that reverence is often lost on fifteen-year-old boys.

I'll have to get after them if they keep it up, but, for now, it's just me and the orange trees.

It's not the right time of year to be pruning them, but the trees were unkept and desperate and I just felt in my gut that it was the right thing to do. Low branches bring disease, and I want to give them a chance to redirect their energy toward growing stronger before winter comes. Besides, the growing season in South Texas is insanely long. Surely, they'll make it to spring.

Okay, maybe I'm not sure if it was the right call or not. So, this is me asking directly. Diosito, please don't let us have our first frost until late January, como el año pasado. Let their roots dig deeper and their branches grow stronger before the danger comes. These trees, they just need a little more time to prepare.

I just needed more time to prepare.

Ah, here I go again. Making another symbol out of my parent's separation.

Back to the simple things. Pruning, praying, planting marigolds.

Pruning, praying, planting marigolds.

Keeping my head above water.

Sol is calling me over.

I'll talk to You again soon.

En el nombre del padre, del hijo,

y del espíritu santo...

I'm so sorry I've been sparse. I know it's been weeks. Things got better, then they got worse, and honestly, I need to learn how to pray outside of the extremes. I'm trying.

Something happened today. I was walking to lunch with Sol, and the topic of Homecoming came up again for the first time since September. We didn't get asked to go by any guys, but that wasn't a surprise. No es nada grave, but it was hard not to feel just a little left out knowing that practically every other girl in our grade will be in attendance.

Sol had a solution. She usually does. She said she would be my date, that we could just go to the dance together.

And that is a totally normal and practical thing to suggest, right? Girls go to school dances with their friend groups all of the time—it just so happens that our friend group is a party of two this time around.

It's just that… I got *really* excited when Sol brought it up. Like, butterflies in my stomach excited. Lightning in a bottle excited. Dopey grin excited.

But You understand, right? I need a win. I need a fun night. What I felt wasn't anything nefarious. Even if Mrs. Perez gave us a dirty look when I jumped into Sol's arms and we almost fell into some bushes, I did nothing wrong. Right?

It'll be fine. And I'm hopeful that it'll maybe even help snap Mom out of the trance she's in. I've never had the school dance experience before, but I imagine it would be a good distraction for her. Between the dress shopping and the salon appointments and everything, maybe it'll push her back into motion.

This is a good thing.

En el nombre del padre, del hijo,
y del espíritu santo…

I'm sorry, I'm sorry, I'm sorry.

Homecoming night was wonderful. I wore a white dress with a halter top and a circle skirt that flared out when I twirled. Liliana styled my cropped hair into bouncy curls. The school photographer said that the look was "very Marilyn." Sol looked dashing in her silky button-down and black slacks. She wore her long, glossy black hair in a high ponytail and I had a fun time playing with it while we waited in line to get punch.

The music selection wasn't great, but that was expected. I didn't really want to dance, since I didn't know most of the songs, but I couldn't stop Sol from dragging me to the dance floor when Mr. Brightside came on. It's a classic, she said. Impossible not to dance to.

And we did.

Diosito, I'm really, really sorry.

I didn't mean to kiss her.

Okay, so I've been mulling this over for hours—painful, confusing hours. But I've come to the conclusion that… maybe it's okay.

Hear me out.

I kissed my best friend. This is fine. I probably should have asked her opinion on the matter beforehand, but her hands were on my waist and her mouth was right there and I was *so* sure that that was what she wanted. What we both wanted.

My best friend is a girl. This is… less fine. Or so I thought. Sure, Catholics aren't exactly known for being particularly open to same-sex relationships, but didn't Pope Francis just say, for like the third time, that homosexuality is not a crime? The Pope is Your voice on Earth. He can't just go off-book like that. His word has to count for something, right?

I kissed my best friend in front of several witnesses. This is bound to have some consequences. But, also, we were just two people in a crowd. The lighting was dark, the hour was late. I bet no one even saw us. And, even if a chaperone did, I don't think they'll do anything too drastic about it. All the guidance counselors know I'm having trouble at home. They'll say this is a private matter if it ever comes up. Definitely.

I'm not dense. I know what most Christians think of gay relationships. I knew what it meant for me the first time that I saw a girl in a plaid skirt and my heart stopped and I pushed the feeling down as deep as it could go. I knew why I ignored it then, and I know why I can't ignore it now. I wasn't raised with fire-and-brimstone Catholicism. Religion has always stemmed from a place of love, from the first moment I learned how to pray.

And You love me, right? You love me how I am. You love me despite my flaws. You love me enough to know that this isn't one of them. This is a good thing. I love You. I think I probably love Sol. How could that ever be a bad thing?

I'm panicking, but I'm fine. We're all just fine.

En el nombre del padre, del hijo,
y del espíritu santo…

In the name of the Father, the Son,
and the Holy Spirit...

I talked to Sol about it and things are so much better than I had expected. She said that she didn't regret the kiss, that she had felt the same way that I did but she didn't want to push anything because of everything that I had going on with my family. Can you imagine? We talked about our feelings and it actually made things better—what a foreign concept.

Thank You, for being here with me. It helps keep everything else at bay.

I was wrong to assume that no one saw us at homecoming. They definitely did. Sol and I have gotten more than a few glances at school today. Still, no one has confronted us about it. Maybe it's too soon to call it, and maybe I'm even being a bit naïve about the situation, but I really think we might make it through this unscathed.

And it's You that gave me the strength for it.

En el nombre del padre, del hijo,
y del espíritu santo...

Things are going to be more difficult than I originally imagined. Mrs. Perez asked me to stay behind after class today. She saw Sol and me at the dance and had some… choice things to say on the matter.

And here I thought we were supposed to love each other. God, I'm exhausted.

The things she said… they made me feel so dirty. She said I was depraved, that I would be the ruin of my family. She spoke of shame. Shame. Shame. Shame.

She made me feel small. She made me feel smaller than small. She made me nothing.

Sinvergüenza, she called me.

Mrs. Perez spent the majority of the lunch period berating me. As my hunger grew, so did my indignation. Because how dare she— how dare she shame me for something kind and light and good? It isn't for mortals to judge. It isn't for us to cast stones. She can't damn me to hell. Only You can do that. And You wouldn't, right? You wouldn't.

You wouldn't.

And still, she invoked Your name. Your wrath. She used every line of the Bible that she could twist into something ugly to let me know that I was cursed. That I had to repent.

I don't... I don't know what else to say. I need her to be wrong. I need You to be on my side, God.

En el nombre del padre, del hijo,
y del espíritu santo...

In the name of the Father, the Son,
and the Holy Spirit…

This is what happened today.

Brother Michael pulled me out of Calculus. Mrs. Perez gave me a stern look. Sol gave me a sympathetic one. I was terrified. I counted every step between the classroom and Brother Stephen's office.

He made me a cup of tea. I watched him pick a mug, set the electric kettle, and offer me his tea selection. When I didn't respond, he chose peppermint. Maybe he meant well. Maybe he wanted me to calm down. But, more than that, I think he hoped I would fill the silence with a confession. So he wouldn't be the one to bring it into the room

I said nothing.

I stared at the mug while he spoke. He asked me if I enjoyed the homecoming dance. I watched amber-green seep out of the half-submerged tea bag, slowly coloring the rest of the water. He asked if I had spoken to my parents about my…distractions. I resisted the urge to shake the tea bag—to make the color spread evenly. He asked me if I had prayed.

I looked up.

He smiled at the acknowledgment. "You're just confused, Camila," he said, not unkindly, "I'm trying to help you."

No, I thought to myself, you are cruel and you are wrong *and you don't believe me.*

For the love of God, somebody believe me.

The love of God... isn't that what got me here?

Isn't Your love what got me here?

En el nombre del padre, del hijo,

y del espíritu santo...

Sol found me after class. If she got the same treatment from the teachers that I did, she didn't let on. I filled her in on what Brother Stephen said as she led me down to the grotto.

I'm praying now, but it's out of habit more than anything. I don't know if there are any answers to be had. I don't know what I would ask if there were.

I can still smell the citrus blossoms. The marigolds are still in bloom. Sol plucked a flower and tucked it behind my ear. She lifted my chin with two fingers and kissed me. In front of Mary and her stoney, serene smile, she kissed me. The earth did not split open and devour us. I felt no fear, just her affection as it washed over my shame.

I cried, but she understood. She held me close until I could almost feel my jagged edges begin to mend.

I'm telling You this, but I don't know what You'll do with it. I don't know much of anything, right now.

I can only assume that Brother Stephen called home after our non-conversation today. Mom was waiting for me in the kitchen. I was happy to see her, at first. It was the first time that she had gotten out of bed unprompted in weeks and, for a second, I thought that maybe it was a good sign.

My hopes were tempered when I saw the grim set of her mouth. The caution behind her eyes as she took stock of me, her youngest child. I saw her take in my short hair, my bitten nails, the rainbow pin on my backpack. I saw her tally it in her head, the signs that maybe she should have known. Maybe she should have intervened.

These are stereotypes. They aren't reasons to assume. Reasons to worry. Except for when they are.

She told me that we needed to talk. And she did, talk— unconcerned with whether or not I was listening.

I tuned in and out of the conversation. In the moments that I was most in my head, I imagined building a wall around myself. I imagined all of the stone that I would put between me and her. The weight of it. The way it would turn her words into a distant echo.

There were moments that I could not help but hear her, my only parent. She told me that, even though things might be difficult right now, it was no reason to act out. She understood that I wanted attention and that I may be harboring some ill-will towards men right now, but that it didn't mean I was a lesbian. Not all men were like my father, she claimed. Not all men would leave. And sinning would only push me further away from You. She said that, worst of all, I was ruining my reputation. All of our reputations.

She said it wasn't worth this. No pride, no show of defiance, and no girl was worth this.

By the end of our conversation, I didn't feel worth much of anything either.

I tried to defend myself to her, but she just held up a hand. She said she wouldn't speak to me until I went to confession.

Sitting alone at the kitchen table, I couldn't shake the image of her silver wedding band, still fitting snugly on the ring finger of her left hand.

What are vows in the face of infidelity? What's blind faith in

the face of a fledgling love story?

God, what is the point of any of this?

En el nombre del padre, del hijo,

y del espíritu santo…

I think that things that are worth doing are worth doing well. Yesterday, when Liliana finally asked me to tend to the garden, I took my time. I donned my gloves and pulled each weed out by hand. No tilling, no trowel. I didn't want to risk breaking up the root systems because that wouldn't help a damn thing. I got on my knees and plucked them out whole—root and stem.

I hate my father well. I'm efficient about it. I hate my father, so I ignore his phone calls. I hate my father, so I boxed up his things and left them on the curb on trash day. I hate my father, so I curse his name every time I walk past his old recliner in the living room. I hate him because I cannot—I will not—hate my mother. No more than I could hate a wounded animal that lashes out with one foot in the bear trap.

Sol waits for me, in the garden. She holds the watering can.

I want to love Her well. I want to love Her gently. I want to take pride in it.

But pride is a sin. And loving Her is a sin.

And yet?

THE RÍO ENTERO

Amoxtli poled the boat across the water sin batallar. Usaba la misma forma que su abuelito taught them when they were young: both feet pressed solidly against the boat, parallel to each other, and using a long wooden palo para empujar against the riverbed—slowly and methodically navigating the chinampas that dotted lo que en algún tiempo era el Río Grande.

It was a cool morning a principios de marzo. El sol, rising steadily over the east, burned away los últimos rastros de niebla that carried over the water. Amoxtli had four children in the boat with them—their two youngest grandchildren, el hijo de un pescador, and a little girl that their neighbor had taken in dos semanas antes. The last child, Marisol, tenía fama de ser bien platicadora, but she only yawned with the rest of them as they skimmed across the green water. That group would be the first of several that Amoxtli would ferry across the water as the day continued.

Como todos los demás en el río, Amoxtli was assigned their rotating occupation on the first Sunday of the month. In theory, it was always something that suited their talents, served their community, and fulfilled them in some respect. Though the new system of labor distribution had existed for nearly fifty years, certain members of Amoxtli's generation se seguían quejando que no era justo, que el sistema no funcionaba, pero Amoxtli had no such complaints. Their routine was a simple one: se levantaba temprano, they brought los chamacos to the water, y les contaba cuentos.

Their primary role was as a teacher—imparting knowledge to the children about the way things were then and what they are now. To teach about progress and destruction and the inevitable push and pull of tides. However, Amoxtli, un poco más romántice que eso, considered themself a storyteller above all else.

They steered the children away from the shore and allowed them to wake up a little more antes de empezar. Xio, la nieta mas chica de Amoxtli, dipped her hand under the surface of the water and y se mojó la cara. The other children laughed and started leaning over the side of the boat to splash each other. Ya pa cuando el barco started to tip over, Amoxtli decided it was time to begin the day's lesson. They sat down on the bench at the prow of the boat, frente los niños, and balanced the pole across their knees.

"Buenos días, chiqititos," they greeted the children, their voice baja y suave. Already, avían barcos de agricultores pasando sobre el agua, tending to the chinampas. Amoxtli took care not to disturb them.

"Good morning, Amoxtli!" the children responded in a chorus.

"Que tal." They smiled. "Do you know why I brought you kids out here en la madrugada?"

"¿Para oír los pájaros?" asked Santi, the fisherman's son.

"To help the farmers?" offered Marisol.

"¿Porque nos odias," grumbled Xio. Her older brother, Mazatl, simply stared at the horizon—still functionally asleep.

"Because today is our first day talking about history. And the history of our people begins here, en el agua." Amoxtli used their pole to gesture out to the water, letting the pointed end of it dip and create ripples across the surface. "¿Qué creen, estan listos?"

All four of the children nodded vigorously. Even Mazatl's interest was piqued.

"Bueno, empezamos al principio. Es importante saber que, over a hundred thousand years ago, toda esta region estaba bajo del agua. It took time, bastante tiempo, pero eventually land rose from the waves. The water remained, though, pooled into resacas and little arroys. However, the Río Grande put them all to shame. It carved through the land, desde las montañas de Colorado hasta el Gulfo. Everywhere that the water crossed, life took hold. Then, about eleven thousand years ago, people started living en estas partes. Vivian del río—they used it for food, for transportation, and as a water source. Nunca, nunca as a barrier, though. They crossed it without fear, as it didn't belong to any one group and was not anyone's to hold."

Xio fidgeted in her seat, growing impatient with the story, "Este cuento ni tiene chiste—that's the same way things are now." She crossed her arms.

"Bueno, you have a point there. Pero things didn't stay like that for long. Soon, the *colonizers* came in and started dividing up the land. First the Spanish, then the Mexicans."

Xio and Mazatl, who had heard Amoxtli speak of colonization before, wrinkled their noses and made the appropriately disgusted remarks. Santi y Marisol, who had not, merely looked at each other in confusion.

"¿Y que—son malos?" Santi asked, "Don't *we* speak Spanish?"

"Si, de una manera," Amoxtli amended, "but that's part of the problem, no? The Spaniards came in and changed the way people talked, cambiaron la manera de vivir. They wanted everything to be the same for everyone, pero para controlarlos, les valia madre la igualdad. They wanted everyone to have the same language, the same religion, las mismas reglas. They had no respect for this," Amoxtli motioned, again, at the water that surrounded them, "no respect for the ebb and flow of the Río Grande, for the way it changed, and asked us to change with it."

"Entonces what did they do?" Santi asked.

"They drew and redrew their borders—the people who lived here were displaced over and over again aunque ni se habian movido. Luego, después del Mexican-American war, they signed Treaty of Guadalupe Hidalgo. En el año 1848, decidieron que Rio Grande iba ser la frontera between the United States and Mexico, instead of the Nueces River. With the stroke of a pen, thousands of people had to decide which citizenship they would keep, qué lado del río they would settle on, qué idioma hablarían sus descendientes."

"But how did they keep people from crossing over anyway?" asked Marisol.

Amoxtli wrinkled their nose, "They built walls, then bridges, y cobraron por el privilegio de cruzar. The natural cycle of people that had endured for generations had to be regulated and monetized to fit into the stagnant world that they created. People *died…*" Amoxtli gripped their pole tightly. "They died trying to get across. Shot dead, right in the water."

Todos en el barco took a moment to drink in the scene in front of them—the river, open and welcoming, with no walls or chain-link fences reflected in the water. Instead, it was surrounded by open fields and tall mesquite trees. All around them, there were signs of life. Peces en el agua y herons waiting for them on the shores, the chinampas floating along the surface of the water, con toda la comida que necesitaban, and farmers en sus barcos tending to them with gentle hands. It was balanced. It worked. It was not what it used to be. After a few more moments, Amoxtli continued their story.

"Time proved that the gringos poisoned what they bought. Por años y años, they polluted the river con maquiladoras and then over-allocated it to water crops that sapped the ground of nutrients. If they had had their way, they would've bled this river dry."

The children leaned in with rapt attention, "What stopped them?" whispered Xio.

"Pos, ustedes saben, nada es eterno—not even an empire." Amoxtli smiled. "By the second half of the 21st century, capitalists on both sides of the 'border' started reaping what they sowed. Particularmente en Los Estados Unidos, climate change wreaked havoc. The West Coast was engulfed in flames, and the East was plagued by hurricanes. By the time the floods started, the federal government was barely getting by."

"Isn't that when like a *lot* of people died? No sé si debes de estar tan… soriente about that." Xio pointed out, her eyebrows bunched together in concern.

Amoxtli dropped the grin, and took on a more respectful tone, "You're right, you're right querida. It was a difficult period, y duro más que diez años. As the sea levels rose and y los huracanes became superstorms, this region was taken back in time. The rivers and resacas overflowed and flooded the land—since we were already at sea level, there was simply no place for the water to go. Everything that was once south Texas and northern Mexico was underwater once again."

"But now we're here," reasoned Santi, "so someone must have fixed it."

"Almost," Amoxtli responded, "nos tardamos, pero eventualmente we figured it out. Those of us who saw our homes destroyed did what we were always meant to do—we followed the course of the water, we adapted. Plenty of people left, but the ones that stayed saw an opportunity. Con los ríos inundados y las rejas torn down by storms, there was no way to tell where the borders were anymore. The governments could have told us, sure, but no one was paying attention to this place. La ecomonía estaba en desarrollo, the population was decimated, and they were too busy trying to save the crumbling cities en el norte y el sur. We stayed quiet, y nos dejaron en paz."

Amoxtli paused their story para parase y to begin pushing the boat forward again, They moved until the boat was lined up con una de las chinampas. Saludaron one of the farmers, who smiled and plucked a few oranges for them from the grove he tended.

Amoxtli peeled an orange as they spoke. "There was still dry land in some places, little islands where we were built permanent structures—granaries to store our food y una biblioteca para los libros that we were able to salvage. The river was wider than ever before, though. Ni podias ver el oto lado. El Río Grande had connected with all of the other resacas and streams in the area and transformed into a delta like nothing anyone had ever seen." Amoxtli distributed the segments of orange between the children, keeping one piece for themself.

"It was difficult, pero we learned." Amoxtli wiped orange juice from their chin with the back of their hand. "We didn't have enough dry land to sow entire fields, so we started building chinampas instead——like the Aztecs did, back in Tenochtitlan. It worked a lot better than we could have hoped, y eventualmente we were able to support ourselves sin tener que pedirle ayuda al gobierno. Food," Amoxtli said, peeling a second orange, "was our first step towards independence."

As the sun started rising higher in the clear blue sky, Amoxtli began steering the boat back towards the shore, aunque le faltaba a su cuento.

"We didn't stop there, though, ustedes saben. Once we got a taste for freedom, nos dimos cuenta de que tanto podíamos cambiar. Como si nada, language began to change. No one cared anymore about 'proper English' or 'good Spanish', si quieríamos comunicar, íbamos a comunicar. We started mixing our languages pos porque que chingados no. It's what made sense, it's what worked. Y si podiamos hacer eso, porque no hacer lo mismo con el género? If language could be fluid, why not gender? ¿Y si el género no tenía que ser binario, porque no cambiamos la familia también? Couldn't family be anyone at all? Nos emborrachamos con todo lo que pudimos cambiar, with everything that wouldn't have to stay the same."

"Okay ahora si nos estás chingando, como que no todos eran familia antes?" asked Marisol, who at eight years old had been raised in more than half a dozen households but thought herself no poorer for it.

"Pos, that's how it was. People had their friends, their 'community,' but they didn't always love each other like family. They didn't share responsibilities como lo hacemos aqui. It was all hierarchical—conditional, even. But when we were building this new community, decidimos que no avía porque hacerlo así. We could share the responsibility, y tambien el amor. We created an extensive foster network para proteger los niños who lost their families in the floods." Amoxtli reached over and brushed a soft brown curl away from Marisol's face. "No child will ever go wanting, here."

The group at in comfortable silence, for a while, listening to the water that lapped against the boat and the pericos chattering overhead. Mazatl groaned, however, when he realized how close they were to the shoreline.

"Already?" he complained, "apenas me estaba despertando de verdad."

"Ya es tiempo, chiqitin. We'll have time for more stories tomorrow. For now, you have chores to do." Amoxtli docked the boat and held each of the children's hands as they stepped back onto dry land. "Bueno, chamacos, what did we learn today?"

"¿Los Españoles son malos?" asked Xio.

"¿Y los Americanos peores?" Mazatl chimed in.

"Oranges are a great breakfast." Santi nodded with certainty.

"Families are bigger than they used to be," said Marisol, "y me gusta mas así," she added.

Amoxtli laughed and kneeled to be at eye level with the children. "All of that is true, yes, y que no se les olvide, but the important lesson is this: things *will* change. You cannot cage a flooding river, but you can learn to move with it when the banks swell. Aunque te calé, you have to learn to trust the tide."

The children smiled and nodded, absorbing what they could of wisdom that they would have to live longer lives to learn themselves. They skipped off into the tall grass, and Amoxtli watched them until they crested a hill and left their sight.

Amoxtli poled back out into the open water, taking a few moments to themself before going to pick up the next crop of children. En un memento de indulgencia, they decided to dive into el río for a late-morning swim. They twisted and turned under the cool water, looking up through squinted eyes to see the sunlight filter down through the surface of the river. When they resurfaced, no sabia if they

were facing el norte or the southern shore.

It did not matter.

Lucia V. Delgado is a Chicago-based writer and educator. She received her B.A. in Honors English from the University of Texas at Austin, where she wrote her undergraduate thesis on language use in borderlands literature. She then moved to Illinois to pursue an M.A. from the University of Chicago. Having been raised on both sides of the Río Grande, and hailing from a family that long predates the border, Lucia wrote *Of the River* in an effort to explain where she comes from.